PIGLET IN A PLAYPEN

"Everyone adores Ruby!" Mandy told Brandon. "She's a real star!"

Brandon laughed. Fondly he tickled the piglet's back. "Tell that to my dad!" he said sadly.

Mandy moved in as his voice dropped to no more than a whisper. "Why? What does he say about Ruby?" she asked.

Brandon gently closed the box lid. "He says she'll have to go!" he muttered. "And since Ken's not around to do the business, it'll be up to me! I'll have to get rid of her," he said.

A shock wave ran through Mandy's body. She stood there in the middle of the classroom, trying to take this in.

Brandon sniffed. "Tonight," he said. "Dad's told me to get rid of her tonight!"

Animal Ark Series

Piglet in a Playpen

Lucy Daniels

Illustrations by Shelagh McNicholas

BARRON'S

All inquiries should be addressed to:
Barron's Educational Series, Inc.
250 Wireless Boulevard
Hauppauge, NY 11788-3917

ISBN 0-8120-9668-1

Library of Congress Catalog Card No.: 96-1848

Library of Congress Cataloging-in-Publication Data

Daniels, Lucy.
    Piglet in a playpen / Lucy Daniels ; illustrations by Shelagh
McNicholas.
        p.   cm. — (Animal Ark series ; 8)
    Summary : Mandy, the daughter of two veterinarians in a Yorkshire
village, hopes to save an undersized piglet from destruction by turning
her into a prize-winning pig.
    ISBN 0-8120-9668-1
    [1. Pigs—Fiction.   4. Veterinarians—Fiction.]   I. McNicholas,
Shelagh, ill.   II. Title.   III. Series : Daniels, Lucy. Animal Ark series ; 8.
PZ7.D2193Pi   1996
[Fic]—dc20   96-1848
                                                                        CIP
                                                                        AC

PRINTED IN THE UNITED STATES OF AMERICA
987654321

Special thanks to Jenny Oldfield
Thanks also to C. J. Hall, B. Vet.Med., M.R.C.V.S.,
for reviewing the veterinary information
contained in this book

One

"Mrs. Ponsonby, this dog is too hot!"

Adam Hope looked up at Pandora's fussy owner. Mandy saw him trying to hide a smile. She was enjoying watching her father at work in the afternoon office hours at Animal Ark. "There's no need at all to be alarmed by Pandora's condition. It's quite simple. She's just too hot!"

Mrs. Ponsonby stuttered and spluttered. "But her little pulse is racing, Mr. Hope! I felt it myself." Her loud, rich voice swelled and filled the treatment room. The silk flowers on her blue hat trembled. "And she can hardly catch her breath. Surely you can see that!"

The hairy little Pekinese dog stood patiently on

the treatment table. She was panting uncontrollably, it was true, and her pink tongue was lolling. Her breath came short and fast.

Mr. Hope swallowed hard and gave a polite little cough. Mandy stood in the corner, smiling brightly.

"Mrs. Ponsonby, how long has Pandora been wearing this padded jacket?" He fingered the straps that fastened the red plaid garment securely around Pandora's rather stout middle.

Mrs. Ponsonby fixed her pink spectacles more firmly on the bridge of her nose and gave the question some thought. "Let me see now. Well, it was my special Christmas present to her this year. She began wearing it the day after Christmas, and the precious little thing adored it from the moment she put it on!" She paused to smile at poor, panting Pandora. "She thinks it makes her look smart, don't you, darling?"

Pandora huffed and puffed.

"And I can say without a word of a lie, Mr. Hope, that Pandora has not parted with her jacket once from that day to this! Except for grooming at the dog parlor in Walton, of course!" She rattled on. "So convenient for keeping off winter chills at home at Bleakfell Hall! Pandora is rather delicate, as you know!"

Mr. Hope got in one halfhearted nod. Mandy

thought of the large vets' bills Mrs. Ponsonby had paid over the years. She certainly cared about her pet, though she sometimes failed to see what was best for her as far as diet, exercise, and now clothing went. Mandy settled her hands deep in the pockets of her white coat and waited to see how her father would handle Mrs. Ponsonby next.

"I always feel that Pandora requires rather special treatment, you know. One can't be too careful!" Mrs. Ponsonby announced. "That's why I'd like you to give her a thorough examination, Mr. Hope. A complete overhaul—heart, lungs...everything!" She gave a delicate pause and the flowers bobbed on top of the blue hat.

Mr. Hope jumped in. "That's not necessary, Mrs. Ponsonby!" He cast a desperate glance at Mandy. "There's nothing wrong with Pandora, I can assure you. She's just overheated!" He began to unbuckle the chic plaid jacket. "You see, we're well into spring now, and Pandora's easily able to cope with the weather." He looked up and gave her a charming smile.

Mandy thought he was managing Mrs. Ponsonby very well. She was relieved to see the little Pekinese shake herself free of the jacket and wriggle her backside delightedly. At last her coat and skin could breathe freely again.

But Mrs. Ponsonby was not convinced. "You mean she doesn't have a heart murmur or anything dreadful?" she asked, hardly daring to believe it.

"No, look! She's already stopped panting. Believe me, Mrs. Ponsonby, Pandora was just one hot dog!"

Mandy gulped and tried not to think of a weiner in a bun with mustard. She enjoyed Mrs. Ponsonby's puzzled silence.

"Tell you what, I'll get a second opinion," Mr. Hope said. He winked at Mandy as he went next door for Simon, the veterinary assistant at Animal Ark.

Simon came in smiling nervously and fixing his round glasses firmly on his nose. He crouched down level with Pandora, inspecting her moist snub nose and wide, dark eyes. He felt the underside of her belly. "Hot!" he commented. "In fact, she's sweating like a pig!"

Mandy heard Mrs. Ponsonby tut-tut with distaste. *Leave pigs out of this!* Mandy thought, but she kept quiet. As far as animals went, Mandy loved them all— rabbits, cats, horses, hamsters, pigs—even Pandora, who was beginning to look restless and bored. Her claws slid and scratched at the smooth plastic table top as she scrabbled to be taken down. She made a little nipping movement with her mouth at the unsuspecting Simon.

"Hey there!" Simon said. He rapidly withdrew his

hand from Pandora's belly, then looked up at her owner. "Fit as a fiddle! Apart from overheating, there's not a thing wrong with her!" he said.

"And that's your professional opinion?" Mrs. Ponsonby persisted.

"It is!" Mr. Hope and Simon said together.

So Mrs. Ponsonby beamed at last and scooped up the precious Pandora into her arms. "There, there, darling!" she sang out. "No more nasty vets for you! No!" And she cuddled the dog in true relief.

"Remember, no jacket for her until next winter's frosts set in!" Mr. Hope said politely as he showed her to the door. "Pandora's sturdier than you think!"

Mrs. Ponsonby nodded slowly as she went. "Better to be safe than sorry, I always say!" she said grandly. She bent sideways and whispered in Mr. Hope's ear, "Nothing's too good for my Pandora!" And she swept out.

Mr. Hope, Simon, and Mandy grinned from ear to ear as the door closed. "A hot dog!" Mandy giggled. She nearly exploded into laughter.

"Shh!" Simon warned. Red-faced, he went back into the residential unit to keep taking temperatures.

"Uh-oh!" Mandy's dad said, holding up the offending plaid jacket. "Mrs. Ponsonby forgot this!" He handed it to Mandy. "Just run along and catch up with her, would you?" he said.

Mandy took it and ran quickly through the busy waiting room out into the small parking area at the side of the building. She saw stout Mrs. Ponsonby leaning into her car to deposit the precious Pandora in the special dog compartment at the back, where Toby, her mongrel pup, sat patiently waiting.

Pandora had already tried to chase off two red setters and a Border collie in the waiting room, and now she set up a loud yapping. James Hunter and Eric, his cat, were just crossing the parking lot.

Pandora seemed to have a new lease on life since her release from the stifling jacket. She barked and bounced madly inside the car at the mere sight of Eric in his basket.

"Mrs. Ponsonby, you forgot this!" Mandy called.

Graciously Mrs. Ponsonby took the jacket. She smiled and waved at Mandy as she got into the car and drove off. Pandora still bounced and yapped in the back.

James shook his head. "It's okay, Eric, you can come out now!" He opened up the flap at the front of the basket and put it on the ground. Eric emerged, keeping a wary eye open for the excited Pekinese.

"Hi!" Mandy knew James had brought Eric in for a routine influenza shot. She was glad to see them both.

Eric was one of the kittens she and James had rescued from Mr. Williams's kitchen at school, and she knew that the Hunters' place was one of the best homes any animal could wish to have. James was almost as crazy about animals as she was, though he hid it better. Sometimes he pretended that football and even computers were more important. But Mandy knew he could never manage to stay away from Animal Ark for long.

"Hi," James answered, ducking his head. His brown hair fell forward across his forehead. He was as shy as always. He bent to pick up Eric.

They stood on the lowest of the three steps that led up to the double glass doors of the office. There was no need to hurry; James was five minutes early for his appointment.

But the doors burst open and a tall, red-faced boy blundered down the steps. He plowed into James and sent Eric leaping off sideways out of his arms in one smooth, liquid movement. James fell backwards into Mandy.

"Hey, watch it!" James shouted.

Mandy scrambled off after Eric and took him carefully into her arms.

The boy took no notice. He muttered something and hurried on down past the house. He went head down, in his T-shirt and jeans, hands thrust deep in his pockets, shoulders hunched.

"That's Brandon Gill!" Mandy exclaimed. She

knew him from school. Everyone knew Brandon.

He lived on a farm somewhere up the valley—a kid who hated school and let everyone know it. He sat at the back in all his classes, usually lounging on the back two legs of his chair, usually staring out the window. He wouldn't talk to teachers. Not many people were friends with Brandon Gill; either they were scared of him or they called him stupid.

"You don't need to tell me!" James grumbled. He rubbed his sore shoulder. "What's he doing here?"

Mandy cuddled Eric and checked to be sure he was okay. "I don't know. He must have come in to see Mom in the other treatment room, but I have no idea what it was about. He's never been here before, as far as I know." She watched Brandon retreat down the road. "It's a mystery to me!"

James was still upset by the clumsy meeting. "No, I mean, what's he doing out? He was absent from school today, sick. He should be at home."

Mandy looked thoughtful. "You know what it's like for farm kids," she said. "If they're busy at home, they sometimes don't show up at school." But she knew Brandon Gill wasn't usually like that. Much as he obviously hated it, he had to go to school and then fit all the farm work around it. "Come on, let's go in and ask Mom!" she decided.

They went inside and found Mrs. Hope talking

quietly at the reception desk with Jean Knox, their receptionist. Mandy's mom had put a brown package down on the desk and seemed to be scratching her head over some problem or other. Jean was looking up information in a file in the drawer behind her.

Mandy smiled at all the people and their pets waiting in reception. She went quietly up to her mom. "Did Brandon Gill just come in to see you, Mom?" she asked.

Mrs. Hope's freckled face was set in a thoughtful frown. "What? Oh, yes. It was quite strange."

Jean rummaged through the file, pulling out cards and then replacing them again. "Gill...Gill," she mumbled. "Graystones Farm...Yes, here it is!" She pulled out a white card in triumph. Then she fumbled for her glasses on a chain around her neck. "Oh, here, you'd better read it," she told Mrs. Hope.

"What was strange about it?" Mandy asked. She felt James at her side, equally curious.

"He's worried about Pauline." Mrs. Hope read the card and pushed one hand through her long red hair.

"Who's Pauline?" James asked.

"A pig."

"A pig!" James's eyes widened and he stared at Mandy. "Brandon Gill has a pig called Pauline?" he asked, astonished.

"Not quite." Mrs. Hope looked up with a friendly smile. "The Gills are farmers, as you know. They keep a herd of pigs. You usually see them up on the slope as you go out of the village through the valley."

James and Mandy nodded. The huge field, with its rounded shelters of corrugated iron where the pigs slept, was a familiar sight. And the smell was instantly recognizable if you got downwind.

"Pauline's a sow who's just farrowed," Mrs. Hope explained.

Mandy saw James's puzzled face. "She's had piglets," she whispered. "Go on, Mom!" Mandy loved to hear all the latest news about births on the farms. She'd never forget being there and helping when two of Lydia Fawcett's goats went into labor up at High Cross Farm. Lydia was an old-fashioned farmer who had only recently begun to make good money out of her goats' milk and cheese, thanks, she said, to Mandy and James. "Tell us about Pauline!" Mandy prompted.

"According to Brandon there are ten piglets. Quite a normal number."

"But?" Mandy stood impatiently waiting for her mother to describe the problem.

"But there's a runt," she sighed. "That's quite normal, too. It's really the runt that Brandon came to see me about. He watched Pauline try to crush it at birth. He had to go in and rescue it."

"Oh, poor thing!" Mandy cried. "Just because it's the littlest one!"

James, too, looked concerned as he held tightly on to Eric. "Is that what they do?"

Mrs. Hope nodded. "Sometimes. But Brandon managed to pull it out of the way. He's called it Ruby."

By now Mandy was completely absorbed in the problem. Brandon—big, tough Brandon Gill—had rescued a runt called Ruby. What would he do now? Would the sow go on feeding Ruby? Or would she refuse to have anything to do with her? "Can the piglet be kept with the mother now?" she asked.

"For the time being," Mrs. Hope said. "Brandon put her back, and Pauline seemed to say, 'Okay, you can stay'!" She smiled and it lit up her green eyes. "But Ruby's not feeding well. She's on a teat at the rear end of the sow, and there's not much milk coming through. So Brandon came in here to ask what he should do next."

Mandy stood and listened. She was kicking herself for passing the time with Mrs. Ponsonby and Pandora when she could have been listening in on this much more serious problem next door. No wonder Brandon looked worried as he hurried off.

"Why didn't he just ask his dad?" James asked in his logical way. "Why did he have to come all the way over here?"

Mrs. Hope nodded. "That's what I wondered. That was the first thing that was strange about it."

"What else?" Mandy asked. Already, and without having even seen the piglet, she cared deeply about the fate of poor little Ruby. She looked anxiously at her mother.

"Well, I was suggesting adding extra food to Ruby's diet. If she's not suckling well, she needs to be weaned quickly. And there are these special pellets." She pointed to the package on the desk. "I was explaining to Brandon and getting the pellets ready for him. I turned my back on him, and he was gone!" Mrs. Hope told them. "Vanished!"

"He ran straight out through here," Jean said, "like a bull in a china shop!"

"And came charging down the steps right into us!" James told them.

"Why didn't he just wait for the pellets?" Mrs. Hope asked. The frown had come back onto her face.

Mandy thought about it. Brandon came to school in fairly shabby clothes, old sneakers and shirts that were frayed at the collar. Some farmers struggled to make ends meet, she knew. "Maybe he couldn't pay for them?" she suggested. "Maybe he got upset and ran away?"

"Hmm." Mrs. Hope nodded. "That's quite likely. You mean he came down on the spur of the moment, not thinking about the money?"

"Yes, then he realized when he was in there with you that he didn't have any money to pay for the food. So he ran out."

"But he must care a lot about that little piglet!" James put in.

There was a long pause, broken only by the meows, growls, and snufflings of the patients in the waiting room.

"I'll tell you what!" Mrs. Hope took a deep breath. "Why don't you take this package of food pellets along to him anyway? We'll worry about payment later."

Mandy's blue eyes sparkled with surprise and delight. "You mean it, Mom?" she said, one hand already around the package.

Mrs. Hope grinned. "Shh! Yes, I mean it, but don't tell anyone! You two run along to the farm. Here, James, give Eric to me. We'll do his shot while you're gone, okay?"

James handed Eric and his basket over the counter. They didn't need to be told again. Mandy led the way out of the office, the package of food under her arm and a happy smile on her face.

James didn't have his bike with him, so they had to

go on foot. They trotted past Mandy's house, under the familiar wooden sign that swung in the breeze and read "Animal Ark, Veterinary Surgeon" in bold letters. Then they were out into the road.

"And see if there's anything else wrong out there at the farm!" Mrs. Hope called out. She'd come around in her white coat to the front of the house. She still looked slightly worried. "I just have that feeling!" she said.

Mandy and James nodded. They'd head straight down into Welford village and then along the riverside to Graystones Farm.

Two

They reached the village crossroads, hardly pausing to say hello to Lydia Fawcett, who was down from High Cross to call in on her old friend, Ernie Bell.

"Can't stop!" Mandy called. She held the piglet's food safely under one arm.

"Another mission of mercy?" Lydia smiled and waved them on as Mandy nodded in reply.

They ran by at a steady trot, straight into a frantic, furry creature straining at its leash.

"Oh, no!" Mandy gasped.

Outside McFarlane's newsstand, Pandora, Mrs. Ponsonby's Pekinese, squared up to Butch, a huge crossbreed dog who lived with Flo Maynard, his owner, in a row house on the main street.

Butch's name was, in fact, misleading. He was the gentlest dog in the village. But Pandora had decided to stop just beside a big delivery van and pick a fight. Mrs. Ponsonby tugged at her leash in vain, while her other dog, patient Toby, sat quietly to heel.

"Shoo!" she said to the huge gray dog. But Butch sat contentedly in the sunshine, his tail going gently from side to side. He cocked his head sideways, his mouth stretched wide, as if smiling. "Shoo! Shoo!" Mrs. Ponsonby waved her free arm at his immovable bulk.

"Come on!" James said. He ran up, with Mandy close on his heels.

"Yap! Yap!" went Pandora.

"Oh, shoo! Nasty big doggie, shoo!" Mrs. Ponsonby wailed.

Butch wagged his magnificent tail and got up to say hello to James.

James hardly had to bend down to give his chin a little scratch. "Hello there, Butch," he smiled.

Pandora panted and strained at the leash.

"Come on, then, boy, come on!" James patted the big dog and led him quietly up his short garden path. He patted him again. Then he rooted around in his pockets and found half a cheese cracker left over from lunch. Butch took it from his palm, gentle as a lamb.

"Oh, thank you so much!" Mrs. Ponsonby exclaimed, red in the face under her brilliant blue

hat. "Poor Pandora! I don't know what we'd have done if you hadn't come along!" The Pekinese had stopped yapping and sat beside Toby, yawning after all her exertions.

Mandy heard, but her mind was elsewhere. She nodded and smiled. James was coming back down Flo Maynard's front path. He closed the iron gate with a firm click. Mrs. Ponsonby was waving, and Pandora trotted meekly beside her into McFarlane's newsstand.

"Mandy, are you okay?" James asked.

"Yes. But I can't get my mind off what Mom said about Graystones Farm. She's sure there's something wrong, and she's usually right about things like that."

James shrugged. "I suppose you want to get a move on." He began to walk ahead. "Come on," he said. "Maybe we shouldn't have stopped to get Butch out of trouble!"

Mandy shook her head. "No, you were great. We didn't lose much time."

They continued on past the newsstand and took a turn down a footpath toward the river. Soon the sweet smells of grass, blossoms on the bushes and flowers in the hedges raised Mandy's spirits.

James decided to jump from rock to rock in the shallows along the water's edge. "Still worried?" he asked.

Mandy shook her head. "No. We'll just deliver these pellets and then we have the rest of the afternoon free."

James hopped nimbly. "Great!"

Soon Graystones Farm came into view. It sat close to the winding river at the end of a long footpath down from the road. The path came up to the house, then cut around the back of the farm buildings. To the three other sides the farm faced out onto large, smooth fields, bright green, yellow and brown. The fields were divided by low green hawthorn hedges or by dark stone walls. They were neat, well-managed fields of wheat and barley, and they ran along the valley bottom as far as the eye could see.

"Where now?" James asked. He jumped up the riverbank and looked towards the plain, square, gray farm building. They had no idea where Brandon would be after his quick exit from Animal Ark.

Mandy scanned their surroundings. The bag of pellets was getting heavy, and she was anxious to make sure the little piglet was fed, but her eye was caught by movements in a distant field. Small black and white smudges roamed about on the hillside, or in and out of tunnel-shaped shelters. "Look!" she said. "Pigs!" Her face lit up.

"Yes?" James said doubtfully. The house was much nearer than the field full of pigs.

"Let's go and look!" Mandy suggested. "Brandon might be up there!" She grinned. She knew that James knew that it was just an excuse. "What do you say?"

James sniffed the air cautiously. "Which way is the wind blowing?" he asked.

Mandy laughed. "The right way!" she told him. She began to skirt the edge of a field, heading up toward the animals.

"What if Brandon's not there?" James asked. He eyed the pigs up ahead suspiciously. Then he came clean. He stopped Mandy by pulling at her sleeve. "Listen," he said. "From what I know about pigs, they can be pretty bad-tempered. My aunt was chased by a pig once!"

Mandy laughed again. "Why, what was she doing?"

"Gathering mushrooms."

"Did the pig get her?"

"Nearly. She dropped all her mushrooms and ran!"

"Clever pig!" Mandy said. "I'll bet he gobbled up her mushrooms. Anyway, we'll be more careful." She paused. "I bet you think pigs are smelly, dirty, disgusting creatures, don't you?" She ran on steadily, keeping the pigs in sight.

"No," James said stoutly. "Okay, then, yes!" he admitted. "I mean, have you ever smelled them from up on the road?" He kept sniffing the wind, dreading the worst.

Mandy breathed in deeply. "A good country smell, as my dad says!" At last they'd reached the field where the pigs were kept. She breathed in again and leaned on the wall to take in the view. Nervously James came up beside her. "Oh!" Mandy cried when she saw the pigs close up. "Oh, aren't they beautiful!"

The Gills' pigs were rooting around in the grass and under the clumps of hawthorn bushes that grew against rocky outcrops in their field. They churned up the soil with their sharp hooves and uprooted big chunks of earth with their snouts.

The biggest of them, a huge black-and-white boar, trundled up and down the hillside, lord of all. The sows stayed closer to their shelters, chomping food at their troughs or lying on their sides to suckle wriggling, squealing masses of pink and black babies.

There were piglets of all sizes everywhere, running, leaping, racing in and out of the corrugated shelters, churning up the soil. It was a warm, sunny day. The land had drained nicely during the fine spring weather. This was pig heaven!

"Look!" Mandy cried. Two sturdy piglets had pulled the same root from the earth and had set up a tug of war over it. Finally the root snapped and sent the two of them toppling over backwards. But each got up and enjoyed half of the tasty treat.

"And look!" James said, beginning to sound more enthusiastic. He watched with awe as the enormous boar approached. His body was a piebald black and white, with one eye sporting a black patch, one eye surrounded by pink. His big, floppy ears fell in his face as he trotted toward them. He seemed almost as wide as he was long, but his little hooves sped daintily over the grass. He approached, nose held high, snuffling.

"Hey, don't they like having their backs scratched?" Mandy said suddenly. She reached for a strong twig, broke it in two and showed it to their enormous visitor. Gingerly she leaned over the wall and scratched the broad back. The pig grunted and pushed up against the stick. Mandy scratched harder. He nosed at her and grunted with delight. "See!" she said.

James nodded. "They don't even smell *too* bad!" he admitted. "Oh, but look! That little one doesn't seem too happy over there." He pointed to a spot about twenty yards away.

A sow lay obligingly by her shelter to let her squealing horde of piglets feed. All but one had a good hold and suckled happily. But whenever the last approached, one of the other, bigger piglets gave it a push or a kick or a shove sideways. And the little piglet went limping off. It looked thin and unhappy, and no wonder!

"I bet that's Ruby!" Mandy breathed. Her heart went out as she watched the miserable runt of the litter wander sadly off. She felt relieved to know that the package of pellets specially for her rested here on the wall. Her mom had been right to send them right up.

And in the distance, at the far side of the field, they saw two people emerge from a stone barn. Each carried a hefty sack balanced on one shoulder, and a full bucket in the other hand. Squinting, Mandy was pleased to see that the taller of them was Brandon Gill.

James and Mandy watched and waited as Brandon and a much older man stopped at each of the shelters on the sloping field. They tipped dried food from the sacks into the troughs and then slopped a milky liquid on top of that. Each time, eager pigs came running. They dug straight into the food in the troughs, noses, hooves, and all.

"Has Brandon seen us?" James asked.

The large, friendly boar had stopped having his back scratched and was ambling up the hill to be fed. Brandon glanced up and noticed him. "Yip, Nelson!" he shouted gruffly. "Here, boy!"

"Yes, he's seen us!" Mandy said with narrowed eyes. "He's just ignoring us! Who's the other man with him? Do you know?"

James rested his arms on the wall. "Ken Hudson, I think. My dad knows him. He plays in the darts team."

Ken was a tiny man, especially alongside lanky Brandon. He was wiry, but he looked lined and old under his flat cap. He was in shirtsleeves and faded brown trousers, with mud-caked rubber boots. Mandy thought he could have been a jockey in his younger days, he looked so lean and scrawny.

"Hey!" The older man nudged Brandon as they reached the lowest troughs with their food and drink. "You have visitors!"

Brandon grunted without looking up.

"Easy now, Pauline! Easy, girl!" Ken talked calmly to the sow as she struggled free of her brood to come up to the trough. He spoke quietly, as if nothing would upset him. He stepped surely among the scrambling offspring. "Do you think you should go over and have a word?" he asked Brandon in the same steady voice, half nodding in Mandy and James's direction.

Brandon ducked his head and went sullen. But there was no way out for him.

"I'll finish up here," Ken insisted. He took the almost empty bucket of milk from Brandon's hand.

So there was no other choice. Brandon stuck his hands in his pockets and shuffled up to Mandy and James.

Three

The wall separated them, and the package of pellets sat on top of it. Mandy noticed that Brandon's severely short haircut made his long neck look longer. His short-sleeved shirt showed his bony wrists. The sun had tanned his face and arms reddish brown. He glowered at them across the wall.

This was really awkward, Mandy thought. She glanced at James. She didn't like the way Brandon stared, and she hadn't liked his rudeness back at Animal Ark. She knew his reputation at school for being unfriendly. Altogether, there was not one likeable thing about this tall, awkward boy, she thought. She pointed to the brown package, aiming to get through this conversation as quickly as possible.

"My mother asked me to bring you these," she said, without smiling.

He frowned back. "What are they?"

"Special feed for Ruby."

"What kind of special feed?" came the surly reply.

"Pellets with extra iron, vitamins, copper, and so on." She shoved the package along the wall toward him. "Mom says she needs them if she's not getting enough milk."

Brandon's frown lifted slightly. He replaced it with a look of puzzlement. "You say she sent them?" he asked. "Without me giving her any money for them?"

Mandy nodded. Brandon stood, legs wide apart, hands still stuffed in his pockets. It was James who broke the stalemate. He jumped up onto the wall, grabbed the package, jumped down into the field, and marched up to the silent, sullen boy. "Here!" he said. "I think we've already spotted Ruby!" He looked sharply around for the thin piglet.

Brandon took the package and opened it. He took a handful of pellets and sniffed at them. "I don't have to pay?" he checked with Mandy.

She shook her head and climbed onto the wall. "Mom thought Ruby needed them right away!" She jumped down beside James.

Ken, the pig man, had been busy all this time, but he looked as if he'd kept an eye on events.

Now he moved off to another shelter.

"What are these things called?" James rattled a fist against the nearest shelter, where Pauline and her piglets still had their feet in the trough.

"Arks," Brandon muttered. He'd gone off down the side of it, making a clicking noise with his tongue. "Ruby!" he called. "Yip, yip! Here, girl!"

"Like Animal Ark!" James exclaimed, with a grin at Mandy. "And what kind of pigs are they?"

"Saddlebacks." Brandon squatted and waited for little Ruby to emerge from her latest hiding place in the shadow of a stumpy hawthorn. She advanced tentatively towards him.

"Poor little thing!" Mandy said. Her mistrust of Brandon was already beginning to vanish. She saw him scoop up the piglet, still just hand-size, and watched as he held her gently under the belly and let her nibble at a handful of pellets. Quickly the little pig gobbled them all.

Brandon looked up at Mandy. "Get us some more of that stuff," he said. "I reckon she likes it!"

Mandy smiled and brought over two more handfuls. "Should I put it down on the ground?" she asked.

"No. Other pigs'll just come and swipe it if you do that," he advised. "Hold your hands down and let her feed."

Mandy did as she was told. The little piglet,

smooth-skinned as a baby, with a poker-straight tail, gobbled every bit of food. Her nose was wet and soft. Mandy heard her sigh with pleasure at the taste of real food.

"There, Ruby! There you go!" Brandon cooed, sounding almost as satisfied. He scratched behind her tiny ear with a long, bony finger. "Hey, Ken, come over here!" he shouted. "And bring that bucket with you!"

The old man came quickly from the next ark, swinging his bucket and whistling. He grinned at James and Mandy. "Nice day," he said.

From close up, they could see the skin of his face was tanned and creased like old leather. There were gaps between his teeth when he smiled. He tilted his cap back and scratched his forehead. "Now then, Brandon, if it's about this little runt you're always talking about—" He began to grumble.

"Just give us the milk, will you?" Brandon interrupted. "I want to see if she can drink from the bucket." Carefully he tilted it sideways until the little pig could reach to sniff at the liquid. She began to nose at it, sputtered a bit, then got the hang of licking and sucking. Soon she'd gulped the milk down.

"See!" Brandon looked up at Ken. "The vet's sent some special stuff for her to eat, and she can manage the milk by herself now!"

"The vet?" Ken said warily. "Does your dad know?"

"We brought it up!" Mandy stepped in to fill the awkward silence. "I live at Animal Ark and I'm a friend of Brandon's at school!" She hoped Ken wouldn't notice how red she'd turned. She flashed Brandon a quick look.

"That's pretty good of you," Ken nodded. Still, he looked down doubtfully at the piglet. "Yep, but she's lost ground," he said. "She's still a skinny little runt!"

Brandon looked hot and bothered, but he didn't have time to answer back. Ruby gave one last snuffle at the milk, backed out of the tilted bucket, and off into the hawthorn bush, her stomach full for the first time in her life.

Mandy and James laughed. "We can bring some more pellets," Mandy offered. "It looks like she'll get through this batch pretty quickly."

Brandon blushed again and stammered.

"It's okay!" Mandy said. She adored Ruby, as she knew she would. "If it's about the money, my mom says not to worry!"

"What do they normally eat?" James asked, quick to change the subject. He saw Pauline emerge from her ark, a contented look on her face.

"This bunch? They eat any old thing!" Ken put in. He laughed. "Worms, roots, acorns, grass, potato peelings, sprouts, cabbage, you name it!"

"It's because they're outdoor pigs—they'll eat anything." Brandon had begun to relax now and offered them information. Once he got going on his favorite subject, there was obviously no stopping him. "Indoor pigs are super fussy, and you have to measure everything—food, temperature, humidity. And then you have to watch for pneumonia. But these, they're as hardy as can be. No fuss. And these Saddlebacks are great for crossing with Large Whites, so you sell them for breeding. We do that with most of our stock."

"Watch it!" Ken said with a laugh. He held on to James as several of Pauline's lively piglets tried to trip him. They seemed to be playing tag around his legs.

James laughed too and stood upright.

"Noisy little pests!" Ken complained. "Now Pauline, old girl, let's get in there to muck you out." He picked up a heavy-pronged pitchfork that rested against the shelter, and he began to clean the ark.

James and Mandy hardly even noticed the smell. They stood watching the piglets' game. Mandy asked Brandon question after question about his pigs. He smiled broadly, taking it easy and leaning against the wall. "People don't know much about pigs," he said. "They talk about 'pig ignorant' and 'dirty pig,'

and that's rubbish. When you keep 'em you soon get to know."

Mandy felt she was even beginning to like Brandon now. "What do you get to know?" she asked. The band of piglets careered up the slope. They tumbled and buffeted each other, squealed and galloped up and down.

"They're really clever!" Brandon said. "And really friendly. And you can train 'em!"

Mandy nodded. But she noticed the boisterous piglets were heading straight for Ruby's hawthorn bush. She pointed. "Brandon, watch out!"

No sooner had she said it than Brandon launched himself up the slope. Ken looked out from the ark and came to see what was going on. Mandy and James began to run after Brandon. It was true—the bullies had found poor Ruby. She squealed as they plowed into her and sent her slithering from her den.

Two piglets pursued her, heads down, butting furiously. Brandon hollered as he ran. Ken raised his fork. Now Pauline had noticed and was trotting to the scene. Worse still, old Nelson had heard the scuffle. He trundled downhill.

"Whoa!" Brandon shouted. He waved his arms to stop the little pigs, then reached down for miserable, bruised Ruby. But too late—another piglet joined in the fun and skipped under his feet. Brandon pitched forward onto the ground. Ruby slipped through his hands and scuttled off, still harried by her bigger brothers and sisters.

And now Nelson's head was down. He hated noise and fuss. He was determined to get in there and sort things out. More than four hundred pounds of solid pig headed straight for Brandon, still splayed full-length on the grass.

"Whoa!" Ken raised his voice. But Nelson thundered on. Ken looked grim. He flung down his fork, grabbed a sheet of wood that stood propped inside the shelter, and stood between the charging boar and Brandon. "Whoa there! Slow down, old boy!" he shouted.

Nelson heard. It was a voice he obeyed. He saw the wooden board, Ken's head poking out above it. He slammed on the brakes, but not soon enough. The slope kept him skidding forwards. Ken held the board up as a shield. Nelson crashed into it. Ken fell back, half hidden by the ark. Nelson rolled downhill with him, stopped, then stumbled to his feet.

Mandy ran to rescue the shivering Ruby from her tormentors. She picked her up and held her own breath. *Please let Ken be all right!* she prayed.

James ran to help Brandon to his feet. They'd heard the crash as Nelson slammed into Ken and he felt the earth shudder as the boar rolled and staggered to his feet. They watched him get up, shake himself, and then trot away. They waited for Ken to get up, too.

All three ran to him, but by the time they arrived, Ken was dragging himself clear of the board. He was conscious, but his thin face was white with pain. "Give me a hand, somebody!" he said grimly.

They pulled him to his feet.

"This leg's bad," he said. He didn't even try to put his weight on his right foot.

"Wait here, I'll call a doctor!" Mandy said. She still held Ruby close to her chest. The poor thing trembled and squeaked.

"No!" Ken said fiercely. "It'll be all right!"

But the boys had to help him out of the field. He slung one arm around each of their shoulders and hopped all the way from the pig field to the house.

They made a miserable procession, James and Brandon on either side of a white-faced Ken, Mandy bringing up the rear with Ruby.

As they finally crossed the yard, a woman came running from the house. Children hovered curiously in the doorway. "Ken!" she shouted. Her dark hair flew back from her face. She wiped her hands on a dish towel as she ran toward them. "What's wrong? What's happened?"

"It'll be all right!" he said through tight lips. Then he slumped forward in a dead faint.

Four

Mandy sat quietly at the table. She was at Lilac Cottage, her grandparents' house, and it was Saturday, the day after Ken Hudson's painful accident.

"What's wrong, love?" Grandad asked with a worried look. "You're not eating your food!"

Mandy looked at the table laden with sandwiches, scones and cherry cake, all her favorites. Usually she could eat her way through any mountain of food that Gran prepared. But today she had no appetite. "I'm not really hungry," she explained.

Grandad shook his head. "That's not like you, Mandy. Are you sure there's nothing wrong? You're not feeling ill, are you?"

But Gran gave him a quick dig in the ribs and rattled off on a different tack. "Let's see, what's new? Oh, your grandad has taught Smoky a new trick." Smoky was another of the kittens Mandy and James had rescued. Everyone had told Grandad that you couldn't really teach cats tricks, but he'd ignored them all. Now Smoky could dribble a table-tennis ball along the lawn and score a goal between two overturned flower pots. He made a pretty good goalkeeper too, nosediving for the ball when Grandad aims a shot.

"Now he can take a tackle and keep possession!" Grandad said, grinning.

Mandy only smiled faintly.

Gran began to look a little concerned. "Let's see, what else is new? Our Women's Institute campaign to save the newsstand is coming along nicely. Everyone wants to sign our petition and keep the McFarlanes where they belong!"

"Good," Mandy said. Then her attention drifted straight back to pigs. She had a vivid memory of poor Ken Hudson collapsing in the farmyard and being rushed off to the hospital. She remembered how Brandon had snatched little Ruby from her and run as soon as his father appeared on the scene. Was that the last she'd ever see of Ruby?

No one had paid the least attention to her and

James as they all crowded around and tried to make Ken comfortable. Mr. Gill climbed into the ambulance with him and drove off. Mrs. Gill went into the house to look after the little ones.

She'd just glanced back at them over her shoulder before she shut the door. "Do you have any idea where Brandon is?" she asked.

James had shrugged and said no.

"What happened?"

Mandy noticed that Mrs. Gill looked suddenly weary. "An accident," she told her. "The pig didn't mean to hurt anyone. It was a pure accident!"

Now Gran cut back into Mandy's thoughts with, "Oh, and did you know that Ken Hudson, the pig man at Graystones, has had an accident and has his leg in a cast? Something happened on the farm, I hear."

Suddenly Mandy snapped into the present. "Yes, that's right!" she said. "How is he?"

"Not too bad." Gran poured more tea and settled down to a good chat. "According to your Jean in reception, who heard from Dora Janeki, who's Ken's older sister, you know…well, anyway, according to Jean, poor Ken was crushed by an enormous brute of a pig that went wild and attacked the poor man!"

Mandy swallowed hard and stood up to keep her grandmother from going on. "Oh, no, that's not right!" she said. "Nelson didn't go wild! He never attacked Ken!"

Gran stopped in her tracks. "Didn't attack...?" She looked puzzled. "Nelson? Are you sure, Mandy dear? Jean is usually so reliable!"

"But you can't exactly say the same about Dora Janeki!" Grandad pointed out. "She does have that little habit of exaggerating and looking on the dark side, remember!" He turned to Mandy. "Anyway, love, no need to upset yourself. Just sit down again and try some of this homemade jam. It's delicious!"

"No thanks, Grandad." Mandy took a deep breath. "But listen, Gran, do you want to know what really happened?" She wanted to set the record straight. "Nelson didn't mean to charge at anybody! He just misjudged his speed, that's all!"

"Easily done!" Grandad nodded. "You have an eyewitness account, eh?"

"That's right. I was there with James. We took some special feed over from Mom. We saw it all!" And she gave them a blow-by-blow account.

Through it all Gran sipped tea and nodded. "How big did you say that pig was?" she asked quietly.

"Oh, he's enormous," Mandy said. "About four hundred pounds."

"And how tall's Ken Hudson?" Gran asked her husband.

"Five foot four, five-five. Weighs about a hundred twenty pounds." Grandpa paused to picture the scene. "By gum, he was brave!" he said. "That's a terrible amount of pig coming hurtling toward you!"

"And after he got hurt he never complained," Mandy told them. "He didn't want any fuss, but he must have been in agony!"

"Well, that settles it!" It was Gran's turn to stand up from the table. Mandy could see that her mind was made up. "Pack up that cake, Mandy, since no one's touched it yet. Wrap it in this foil; that's a good girl. We'll take it right over and pay Ken a visit. Poor guy, he'll need people to cheer him up!"

"Why, where is he? Is he still in the hospital?" Mandy scrambled to do as she was told. She stood ready by the door.

"Oh, no, much worse than that, dear!" Gran said with a faint smile. "They kept him overnight for observation, but they discharged him this morning. No, he's had to go to stay with his sister until the leg gets better."

Mandy saw her grandfather's face drop. He took the keys to their van from his pocket. "I've just remembered my tomatoes," he mumbled. "Very important stage in the greenhouse...watering... feeding...pollinating...! Here, you two don't mind going to visit old Ken by yourselves, do you?"

He handed Mrs. Hope the keys and scuttled out through the back door. "Have a good visit. See you later!" he called.

Mandy opened her eyes wide. "Why, what's wrong with Ken's sister?" she asked.

Gran pursed her lips. "Dora Janeki? Nothing, really. Nothing at all!" she replied.

Dora Janeki stood at her faded green front door, arms folded, a virtual copy of her brother Ken. She was a tiny, skinny woman with gray hair pulled straight back. Her face was wrinkled like an old apple, and all her features were sharp: sharp nose, sharp eyes, sharp elbows. She was all angles and corners, and she greeted Gran and Mandy in a sharp, high voice.

"Oh, it's visitors, is it!" she said shrilly. "Did he know you were planning to come and see him?" She barred the door in her dark working clothes.

"Well, no, not exactly," said Gran. She faced up to Mrs. Janeki. "But Mandy here was telling me all about his accident. We thought we'd just pop over and cheer him up a bit."

Dora Janeki's sheep farm stood on a barren field, three miles from Welford village. It was a windswept, shabby place and had a miserable owner to match. Up here two things were certain: the wind always blew and Dora Janeki never smiled.

"Oh," she snapped, "It'll take more than that to cheer him up. He's at death's door, you know!"

Mandy frowned, but Gran winked at her.

Mrs. Janeki moaned on. "It's a broken leg, they say, and it's a miracle that it's no worse. But who's to say there are no hidden injuries? Internal injuries? The hospital says he has to take things very carefully!"

"Well, we've brought him a cake!" Gran said, determined to sound cheerful. She pointed to Mandy's foil-wrapped package.

"Did I hear 'cake'? Who's that, Dora?" a voice called from inside. Mandy recognized Ken's kindly tone.

"Hello, Ken!" Gran cried. "How's the invalid?" She outsmiled Dora Janeki's frown and strode in to see him. Mandy plucked up courage and followed.

The room was dark and old-fashioned. Ken was propped up in a flowered armchair. His right leg was stretched straight out on a wooden chair, with a snow-white plaster cast from toes to knee. Still he managed a smile as they came in. "Hello there, Dorothy!" he said bashfully. "And who's this you've brought with you? Isn't this the young lady who saw me get my comeuppance yesterday afternoon?"

Mandy grinned. She decided she liked little Ken Hudson.

"Wounded soldier," Gran smiled. "I've never known you to take time off work, Ken!" She drew up another chair. "This is my granddaughter, Mandy," she told him proudly. "She's been busy defending that pig that did all the damage, I'm afraid!"

Ken laughed. "You hear that, Dora? I tried to tell you it wasn't Nelson's fault!" he cried.

His sister came grumpily into the room. "Hmph!" She thumped the cushions behind Ken's back and rattled a poker against the hearth. A smoldering coal fire came back to life "I'm just saying a man your age shouldn't still be messing around with pigs!" she snapped.

Ken sighed. "Maybe a younger man would have jumped out of the way, right enough." He shook his head and stared unhappily at his injured leg.

"Oh, no!" Mandy reassured him. "Nelson was galloping full speed. I doubt if anyone could have jumped clear!"

Ken nodded and his face brightened.

"*And* you saved Brandon from being trampled underfoot, remember!" Mandy said.

"Oh, that!" Ken said modestly. Then he turned to Gran. "Now, that's what's really worrying me," he confided. "Young Brandon and those pigs!"

"What about young Brandon?" Gran asked.

"Well, I'm laid up here for a good few weeks, the

doctor tells me. And it couldn't have come at a worse time. David Gill's going under already, without me being off work. And he's been carrying on a lot lately about the pig herd, how it's not paying its way and how he has too many forms and whatnot to fill in as it is, without worrying about extra work they're bringing in on quotas and regulations and such!"

Dora cut in with a huge sigh. "Don't talk to me about regulations!" she moaned.

"No, well, David has no time for the pigs, if you want to know the truth. He leaves everything to me and that eldest boy of his!"

"Brandon?" Mandy asked.

"That's him. Mad about pigs, he is. Always out on that field tending them. I can't keep him away!"

"Then surely he's a good person to take your place while you're off?" Gran suggested. "And there's no need for you to worry!"

"Ah!" Ken shook his head. "He can look after them as well as me...almost!" He gave a wink. "No, that's not what's worrying me."

"Well then, what?"

"It's me being off work all this time; I'm afraid it might be the last straw as David sees it. He won't see that the boy can do the job properly. He's a bit shortsighted that way, David is!"

Mandy felt a sudden strong pang of sympathy for

Brandon. His father didn't trust him. Yet she'd seen him working with the pigs and knew he was good.

"Well," Ken went on, "me losing my livelihood is one thing. I'm an old hand, and some people say I'm ready to be put out to pasture!" He raised his hand before Gran or Mandy could object. "But those pigs are Brandon's whole life. I can see David wanting to get rid of them while I'm laid up, and it'd break the boy's heart, believe me!"

If Mandy needed convincing that what Ken said was true, the proof came the following Monday while she was helping with evening office hours at Animal Ark.

Mrs. Hope was on duty, calm and collected as usual, and they were winding down after her treatment of a case of mange in a farm dog. "A nice gentle session!" she said as she removed her gloves. "And time for a cup of tea!"

She leaned out and glanced around the empty reception room. Jean was locking cupboards and file drawers. Mandy looked out into the parking lot to check they had no more patients to see to. "Uh-oh, I think you spoke too soon!" she said.

Brandon Gill had flung his bike down on the gravel and was racing up to the door. Something bulged and wriggled inside his faded gray zip-up jacket. He burst into the office, his face desperate.

"It's Ruby!" he gasped. "Will you have a look at her?"

Mrs. Hope glanced quickly at him and then ushered him through into the treatment room. "Come on, Mandy," she said. "I expect we'll need some help!"

Once inside the room, a breathless Brandon unzipped his jacket. The little piglet crouched in a sling that he'd made out of a piece of rough cotton cloth. It hung over one shoulder and down his front in a kind of loose pouch. They could hear Ruby whimpering from inside her warm refuge.

"What's the problem?" Mrs. Hope went over and offered to lift Ruby out onto the table. She smiled

down at the little blunt snout and soft, floppy ears. "What a nice little pig!" she said. "Let's see, what have we here, exactly?" She set Ruby down. "British Saddleback variety. Just weaned, by the look of her. Well done, Brandon." She smiled at him. "Hardy outdoor type, early maturer. A bit underweight. The runt of the litter." She looked Brandon directly in the face. "Did you do all right with those enriched pellets?"

Brandon nodded. "She's been a champion. Can't get 'em down her fast enough."

"So why did you bring her?" Mrs. Hope bent down for a closer look.

He stammered out his explanation, looking to Mandy whenever he got stuck. "She can't put that back leg down right, see! I found her being beaten up by the others again, only I didn't get in there quickly enough this time, and they really went at her. When I did get rid of them, she was pretty bashed around. There's a bite on her back there and she was squealing like mad—and now she can't walk!"

"And you're afraid the leg's broken?" Mrs. Hope asked. Quietly and confidently she took the piglet in one hand. With the other she gently felt the length of the affected leg.

Mandy held her breath. She could see Brandon

had turned white as a sheet.

At last Mrs. Hope looked up. "Well, you can both breathe again!" she announced. "Ruby's leg is badly bruised, but not broken. It's a bit swollen below the joint here, but the bone's definitely still in one piece, you'll be glad to know!"

Brandon's face broke into a smile. He could hardly keep himself from jumping in the air. "It'll mend then, and she'll be able to walk okay?"

"Oh, yes. But..." Mrs. Hope began a serious warning. "I don't give much for Ruby's chances if you keep putting her back with those others. They'll just keep picking on her if you do!"

Brandon's face fell again as Mrs. Hope offered him the piglet. He put her back in the sling.

"I mean it, Brandon. It's tough for a 'tail-ender' like Ruby. You know, the one who gets the worst position for suckling, the little puny one. It's nature's way for them to gang up on her. And in the end they could kill her!"

Brandon hung his head. The piglet was already nestled up against him. "Yes, I know," he said quietly.

"You've seen it happen?" Mrs. Hope asked.

"Many times," he agreed.

"So you know I'm right. You'll have to take her out of the litter and hand-rear her. No putting her back this time!" Mrs. Hope went to wash her hands, sounding brisk. "And of course there's no reason why Ruby won't grow into a strong, healthy pig if you do what we're saying. Keep on feeding her the special pellets, and there'll be no problem." She smiled as she showed him to the door.

Mandy decided to walk out with him to where his bike lay in the parking lot. "Nothing's broken," she reminded him. "That's a relief."

Silently he zipped up his jacket. She bent down and picked up his bike for him. He looked up at the blue sky flecked with white clouds. He managed a tiny nod.

"So what's wrong?" Mandy asked quietly.

He got astride the bike and glanced quickly at her. "You all think it's easy," he said. "Just keep her separate. Hand-rear her! Nice and simple!" He gritted his teeth. Mandy heard a tiny snort from Ruby. "But you try telling that to my dad!" he muttered as he finally pushed off. "Pigs mean money to my dad, and that's all! If they don't pay he won't be bothered with 'em!"

His head went down and he started pedaling down the road. "No, if my dad finds out Ruby needs special treatment, that'll be the end of it!" was his final word.

Mandy remembered David Gill's stern face and Ken Hudson's comment, "It'd break the boy's heart!"

She felt unusually touchy as she went back inside. It was that old feeling of helplessness and a fear that Ruby might have to suffer through no fault of her own.

Life isn't fair! Mandy thought as she scrubbed and disinfected the tables. *Life just isn't fair!*

Five

Brandon took Ruby home, and Mandy heard no more. But next day at school it looked as though he'd decided to take it out on the whole world.

Mandy watched him play in a soccer match during lunch break. He booted a dirty soccer ball up the field, kicking it as if he hated it. He defended the goal as if it were a war zone, seeing off attackers with reckless headers and headlong tackles. And he crouched between the goalposts, frowning, ready to pounce. Today nothing would get past him.

James dribbled the ball back upfield for the opposing team. He brought it into the penalty area, dodging skillfully, his brown head bobbing and weaving through boys much bigger than he. The only way he could be stopped now was by a foul. Sure enough, Mandy saw James feet chopped from under him by a desperate defender.

"Penalty!" the referee declared.

Mandy felt the tension rise as James placed the ball on the spot. He prepared to take the kick. In goal, Brandon clapped his gloved hands together then took up his goalkeeper's crouch. He glowered at the ball, his mind fixed on saving the shot. James backed off, studied the goal, looked down at the ball, and began to run. Mandy held her breath. She wasn't sure if she wanted James to score or Brandon to save it. James's foot made contact. He belted the ball low and hard toward the corner of the net.

Brandon dived. The ball thudded into his outstretched hands. He grasped it. Saved! But Brandon took the back-slapping congratulations of his teammates grim-faced. James shrugged and ran up the field, head down.

"Never mind," Mandy told James at the end of the match. "The way Brandon looks today, nobody could score against him!"

They watched his tall, lonely figure lope off the field ahead of everyone else. Mandy jogged up to the school alongside James.

"Come on!" James put on a burst of speed. "Let's

go and ask him how Ruby is!"

Mandy smiled. That was one of the things she liked about James—he never sulked.

"Good save!" he told Brandon. Other players and spectators jogged along with them. Inside, a bell had sounded for afternoon classes.

Brandon gave one nod of his head. He looked as if his team had lost, not won, Mandy thought.

"How's Ruby today?" James asked as they approached the locker room.

The question stopped Brandon in his tracks. All the other kids piled past them through the door, flushed with success or shrugging off defeat. "She's okay," he muttered.

"But?" Mandy asked. She'd caught that dismal note in his voice. She waited impatiently for him to go on.

"I said she's okay!"

"So why the long face?" she demanded. "What's the matter now?"

"Nothing! It's not me and it's not Ruby!" Brandon nearly bit her head off. "Now just leave us alone, will you?" He turned to rush inside.

"It's your dad, then, isn't it?" Mandy guessed. She wasn't prepared to let this drop; Brandon's bad mood wasn't going to put her off.

Again he stopped dead. "Yes!" he growled. "If you have to know, he caught me bringing Ruby back on the bike after I'd left your place!"

"And you could tell him there were no bones broken, couldn't you? That soon she'll be good as new?"

Brandon nodded sarcastically. He bent to push his long socks down around his ankles. "Oh, yes! But he saw right away that she was underweight. He never bothered about the limp. A limp doesn't affect how much she's worth, does it?"

Mandy and James backed off, a bit afraid of his anger. "So what did he say?" James asked.

"He said straight out, 'Well, she's no good to me. She'll never make up the lost weight!' That was it, word for word, okay?" Brandon's voice had gone flat and hard. He turned his back.

"Meaning what? What did you do then? Where's Ruby now?" The questions tumbled from Mandy's mouth.

"It's okay, don't panic." Brandon had pushed the locker-room door half open. "I told you she was safe, didn't I?"

"Yes, but what did you do with her?" Mandy knew Ruby couldn't be out in the field with the rest of the pigs.

"I brought her with me," he said simply.

"You brought her into school!" James half shouted. Two girls stared at him as they went by. "Ruby's here in school?"

Mandy felt her mouth drop open. "So where is she?" she gasped. A pig wasn't an easy thing to keep quiet inside your bag or to hide in your locker!

"She's in the biology lab," he explained, as if it was obvious all along. "I asked if I could keep her there until this afternoon. I'll tell you later!"

"Today we have something a bit unusual!" Mr. Meldrum began his English lesson by perching on his desk. He hitched his trousers clear of his ankles, pausing to let the class settle. "It's a last-minute arrangement, but I've agreed to go ahead with it and trust to luck!" He smiled uneasily.

Mandy sat near the front. She had to twist around to try to see what he was talking about. Everything was normal at the moment, she thought.

"Now, some of you may have noticed," Mr. Meldrum went on, "That Brandon Gill isn't in his seat."

"Is he under the table, sir?" a joker called out from behind his hand. A laugh rippled around the room.

The English teacher cleared his throat. "I'll ignore that, Justin!" he said. "When Brandon does arrive, you'll soon see what I mean by this being an unusual lesson. He's going to give us all a talk as part of his oral assessment, and I want you all to give him every consideration!" He looked sharply around the room, dwelling on the people sitting giggling at the back. "Remember, hardly anyone enjoys standing up to give these talks, but it's something you all have to do eventually!"

"You mean to say Brandon Gill can talk!" a cruel voice cried out.

Mandy felt like jumping up. But Mr. Meldrum fixed his eye on the culprit. "That makes it your turn tomorrow, Becky, all right?" He turned away and continued to prepare them for the lesson. "Remember, the subject you choose is up to you, but you must talk clearly, with interest and enthusiasm, for a full ten minutes. I know many of you up till now have chosen popular music, or a TV series, or perhaps computers."

Mandy sat with a peculiar feeling creeping up on her that she knew exactly what Brandon's talk was going to be about. And it wasn't video games!

"But Brandon's subject may surprise you," he went on. He paused again to hitch himself off his desk. "Ah, here he is now!"

He went to open the door for Brandon, who entered awkwardly. He carried a large cardboard box, was very red in the face, and looked as if he wished the ground would swallow him up.

Mandy blinked hard. She knew now that she was right. She waited to see how the rest of the class would react.

"Ready?" Mr. Meldrum asked Brandon, who put

the box on the desk and stood in agony in front of the blackboard.

He gulped and nodded.

"All right, everybody! Brandon's here now, and he has ten minutes to tell you all about pigs!"

Mandy felt the stunned silence. She saw the cardboard box rock slightly, and she heard a miniature snort from inside.

Brandon began slowly with a choked voice and a wild, desperate look in his eye. "There are eight hundred million pigs in the world," he croaked.

"And there are eighty named breeds, including Large Whites, Welsh, Landraces, Berkshires, and Gloucester Old Spots." He gave the list in a flat monotone. "You call a female pig a gilt before she has any young, and you call a male pig a boar."

"I call *you* a bore!" someone else choked.

Mandy heard the stifled giggles. She only hoped Brandon hadn't noticed.

"Shh!" warned Mr. Meldrum.

Brandon went frantically on. "The History of the Pig!" he announced. "Pigs lived in woodlands in Roman Britain, and right through Saxon and Norman times." He stumbled over words and blushed redder and redder.

This is torture for him, poor guy, Mandy thought

"They roamed wild and foraged for their food

until the sixteenth century. Then they were kept from Tudor times in sties."

"What's in the box, sir?" someone called impatiently. "Can't he just open the box?"

"Carry on, Brandon," Mr. Meldrum said evenly. "You're doing very nicely!"

The box rocked and the snuffling grew louder.

"Pig Farming Today!" Brandon announced. Panic was still written all over him. "Pigs must be kept in peak condition by the right amount of food, heat and light. The sow breeds all year round and is pregnant for a hundred and fifteen days. She has around eleven to twelve piglets, and each one should weigh about three and a half pounds at birth." The facts came out mechanically, but he knew his stuff, all right.

Mandy noticed that the whole class had settled down and begun to listen. Brandon's voice had stopped croaking and choking; he was getting into his stride. She began to breathe more easily for him.

"Piglets are born with sharp teeth," he said. "We have to trim these to keep them from harming the sow. She can suckle them for fifty-six days. She's usually allowed to have six litters over two and a half years." He paused for breath.

"Quite often the last piglet to be born is shoved out by the sow. Then sometimes this runt of the litter is bullied by the other piglets!" Carefully Brandon opened the flaps on top of the box. There was a rustling of straw as he delved inside; then a gasp ran around the room. Ruby emerged into the light, her legs going like windmills. But Brandon held her safe in his firm and gentle grasp.

"Aah!" voices whispered. "Isn't it sweet!" There was a general air of excitement. The atmosphere of the room was transformed.

"Ruby is one of those special pigs," Brandon explained. He kept her cradled in his arms. She peeped curiously at the class full of beaming faces, her own little black face cocked to one side, ears

flopping. "She was the rear-ender, and she didn't feed well. Pigs can put on over a pound in just one day, but Ruby didn't do anything like that. So I had to take her out and give her special food to help her put on the weight." He glanced gratefully at Mandy. She smiled back. "Well, you can see she's doing great now!"

He looked up proudly, and Mr. Meldrum nodded his approval. "Good! Now, any questions for Brandon?" he asked.

Hands shot up. "Yes, sir! I want to know, can you show pigs like you can sheep and cows and other animals?"

Brandon nodded. "Course you can. Pig shows happen all over. You have to shampoo and groom the pigs, and you have to train them with a stick and a board so they don't just wander off." His face relaxed as he demonstrated how to hold the imaginary board. His subject had taken him over, and he actually seemed to be enjoying himself! "You can't put a collar or a harness on a pig," he explained.

Meanwhile he sat Ruby on the wooden floor, and she looked curiously around at the forest of legs and feet.

"And why do pigs have curly tails?" someone else asked.

Brandon paused. "Don't know. Never thought

about it," he admitted.

"Can I pet Ruby?" Becky asked from the back row. She moved forward with one arm outstretched and made small tweeting noises with her lips. Her face screwed up with delight as Ruby allowed her to tickle her back. "She's so silky and sort of...solid!" she whispered.

Ruby's confidence grew. She stood up on her dainty hooves and began nosing down the aisle between rows of desks.

"Is she all right?" Mr. Meldrum checked with Brandon. The little black-and-pink pig sniffed delicately at people's shoes and nibbled a lace.

"As long as no one makes her jump," he said. "She always was a nervy little so-and-so!" His face was happy, relieved. Mandy felt herself warm to him and Ruby all over again. "I took to her right from the start," he explained. "Because she was so friendly and outgoing. She'll go up to anybody!"

Mr. Meldrum smiled back. "She's great! And what qualities do you think it takes to look after a pig like Ruby?" he asked.

Brandon considered it, thumbs hooked into his trouser pockets. "Patience, mostly," he said. "Pigs like you to be quiet with 'em, and they like to be cleaned out regularly, so you need someone who'll do that right." He paused again and bent to pick up Ruby as she wandered past Mandy back to him. "I dunno; you just have to like 'em, really!"

Mr. Meldrum beamed and began the applause. The whole class clapped for Brandon and Ruby. Mandy sat in her seat almost choking with happiness for them. She clapped and clapped.

Then it was time to pack up and see Ruby safely into her box. Mandy went to help Brandon sort out the straw. "Everyone adores her!" she told him. "She's a real star!"

Brandon laughed. Fondly he tickled Ruby's back. "Tell that to my dad!" he said sadly.

Mandy moved in as his voice dropped to no more than a whisper. "Why? What does he say about Ruby?" she asked.

Brandon gently closed the box lid. Chairs scraped all around them, and the door opened and closed as people left. "He says she'll have to go!" he muttered. "And since Ken's not around to do the business, it'll be up to me!"

"What does he mean, 'She'll have to go'?"

"I'll have to get rid of her," he said, barely audible. A shock wave ran through Mandy's body. She stood there in the middle of the classroom, trying to take this in.

Brandon sniffed. "Tonight," he said. "Dad's told me to get rid of her tonight!"

Six

"No way!" Mandy told James.

They met up after school, out on the empty soccer field. Brandon stood miserably clutching his cardboard box, Ruby nestled snug inside.

"You don't know my dad!" Brandon reminded her. "He means what he says!"

"What is he, then—some kind of monster?" Mandy flung her arms wide. "How can he sentence a poor piglet to death without even a second thought?" She stood there on the field, blue eyes sparking with anger.

"Can't you change his mind?" James asked.

Brandon stood shifting from foot to foot, head down. His victory in the English class had soon worn off. "You don't talk to my dad about stuff like that," he muttered. "He'd just say you were soft and tell you to get on with it!"

"You're not soft!" Mandy protested.

"I know I'm not. Usually I would know not to kick up a fuss. But there's something special about Ruby."

"There is!" she agreed. Little pink-and-black Ruby with the appealing face and dainty hooves.

"So what can we do?" James asked.

"Well, we're not going to get rid of her, that's for sure!" Mandy said with a shudder. She peeped into the box. "You hear that, Ruby? You're safe with us!"

Ruby squirmed deeper into the straw and snored.

Brandon laughed in spite of everything. "She doesn't care!" he said. "She's fast asleep!"

"So what are we going to do?" James insisted. He looked anxiously at Mandy.

"Hide her!" she said simply.

"Hide her?" Brandon and James repeated.

Mandy tried to pull herself up to Brandon's height. "Yes, hide her!" She stood to attention. "Operation Saddleback. Mission: to rescue Ruby! Aim: to keep her hidden from your father! Method: to hand-rear a perfect pig!"

The others nodded slowly.

"Where do you hide a pig?" James dared to ask

the obvious question. Ruby snored loudly inside her box.

"Yes, I had to bring her into school today to keep her out of my dad's way. It's that bad!" Brandon reminded her.

"Details!" She waved a hand airily. "Let's not get bogged down in details of where and how. First off, do you agree we have to do something?"

"Yes!" they said wholeheartedly.

"Right then. Move number one: Animal Ark!" And Mandy strode across the field toward the school gate.

Brandon's long stride easily kept pace, but James had to half run so that he could talk to her. "Can we drop the army routine?" he pleaded. "All this stuff about missions and operations makes me nervous, okay?"

"Okay," she agreed. "I'm only doing it because I'm nervous myself!" She looked sideways at them both and felt she'd better explain. "We're going to stop off at Animal Ark for more food for Ruby," she said. "If we're really going to hide her, she'll need a whole stack of those pellets, won't she?"

Brandon nodded and went red in the face. But he looked determined. "I can pay for them this time," he said.

"Oh, no—" Mandy began.

"Yes!" he cut in. "Since Ken got hurt, Dad's agreed

to pay me to do the pig work for him." He looked proudly at Mandy and James, his dark brown eyes steady and serious. "So I can pay for Ruby's feed from now on!" he insisted.

He mounted the school bus, box under one arm, with the same firm, sure look and a quick wave.

"Meet you at Animal Ark!" James called as he and Mandy went for their bikes.

"Whose pigs are these?" Mr. Hope sang out, full-voiced, as if he were in the church choir. He stood admiring little Ruby, who stood on the treatment table. His lips imitated a trombone tune, then he belted out the song once more:

"Whose pigs are these?
Whose pigs are these?
They are John Potts',
I can tell 'em by the spots,
And I found 'em in the minister's garden!"

"Dad!" Mandy protested. He could be so embarrassing!

"What? Don't you like that song?" he asked with a grin, miming a trombone player. "Well, she's a very cute little thing, isn't she?" he said, studying Ruby.

"Not so much of the 'little,' Mr. Hope!" James reminded him. "We're trying to fatten her up, remember!"

"Oh, yes, sorry, James!" Mr. Hope nodded. "That's a very *sturdy* little—I mean...a very *strong, sturdy* piglet you have there, Brandon!"

"Thanks!" Brandon grinned back. "And how much do I owe you for the feed?"

Mr. Hope gave a wave, then scratched Ruby on the back. Ruby sighed. "Oh, let's talk about that later!" He picked up the piglet and set her down on the floor in front of a hefty pile of pellets and skim milk. "Food time!" he encouraged. He folded his arms and watched with a lopsided smile. His dark beard made him look warm and friendly—a vet you could talk to.

Brandon cleared his throat and put one hand in his pocket. "I'd like to settle with you now, if that's all right, Mr. Hope," he insisted.

Adam Hope glanced at Mandy, who gave a tiny nod. "All right then, if you just go and check with Jean out in reception about how much you owe us, I'll keep an eye on Ruby in here!" He smiled at Brandon. "He seems very fond of the little thing!" he said quietly to Mandy and James.

Mandy nodded and sighed. "He is."

"But his father isn't!" James explained.

"Aha!" Mr. Hope said quickly. "I spy another rescue operation! Am I right?" He studied Mandy's reaction.

"Operation Saddleback," she replied. She felt her face settle into a frown. There was no putting it off any longer; they must get Ruby up to Graystones Farm and find her a safe hiding place. She watched as Ruby stepped neatly out of the empty metal dish and licked her broad snout clean. "Come on, girl!" she said, picking her up and putting her back inside the freshly lined box. Ruby wriggled and gave a definite oink! "Time to go home!"

"Brandon! Brandon!" Three little Gills rushed toward them across the farmyard. They were smaller versions of Brandon—dark-haired and skinny, all legs and arms. They flew at their big brother in delight.

One by one he picked them up and swung them around. One by one he set them down and watched them stagger in dizzy circles.

Mandy looked wide-eyed at James. Was this the rough, tough, surly Brandon Gill of Walton Moor School?

"More!" the children clamored. A farm dog leaped out of a nearby barn and yapped madly. "More, Brandon!" They raised their arms to be held and swung.

Brandon obliged, swinging them around and holding them steady as they swayed. He ruffled their heads and patted the rough-haired dog and watched them all run crazily around.

"What's in the box, Brandon?" the biggest girl clung to him and demanded. She was about seven, gap-toothed and freckled.

"What box are you talking about, Angela?" he asked, making grand gestures and shrugging and shaking his head. But there was a panicky look in his eye. "I don't have a box!"

"Yes, you have!" Angela swung her ponytail and pulled at his blue school sweater. "I saw you with it from the window!"

"Pig food!" Mandy came in quickly. "We've put it away now!" It was half true; the extra bags of food were stacked alongside Ruby in the heavy box, which was now safe in a corner of the hay barn.

"Aah!" was Angela's disappointed reply. She immediately lost interest and came to stare at James and Mandy.

Shyly Brandon introduced them to Angela and the little twins, Christopher and Lola. "Mandy lives at the vets' house at Animal Ark," he told them. "She's come to see the pigs."

"Who wants to see rotten pigs?" asked Angela in disbelief.

"We do!" Mandy told her. "We think they're great!"

Angela obviously thought she was crazy. She went up to James instead and put a hand into his. "Come and see Harry," she said.

"Who's Harry?" James looked at Mandy, trying not to grin.

Angela's brown ponytail swung as she turned away. "My gerbil," she said, straight-faced. "He's just had babies!" And she led James into the house.

Brandon shrugged. "I did try to tell her," he explained, blushing as usual. "I said she should call it Harriet."

Mandy laughed. The twins found a hand each. Their plump little fingers grabbed Mandy firmly and their spare thumbs went into their round, red mouths. They stared up at the newcomer.

This is not finding a safe place for Ruby! Mandy told herself impatiently. The black-and-white farm dog, not wanting to be left out, jumped up against her chest, wagging her tail furiously.

"Down, Maggie!" Brandon ordered. "We'd better take the twins inside and then get going," he told Mandy, with a nervous glance back at the hay barn.

So she followed him into the big, square kitchen, already pleasantly surprised by the family living at Graystones Farm.

The kitchen was like the children—a higgledy-piggledy mess of tables, chairs, cushions, toys, half-eaten cakes and cookies, abandoned cups of juice and dish towels drying by the stove. It had oak beams and a stone floor, but still it didn't look like a museum.

It was cozy and lived-in. Mrs. Gill stood by the stove, tasting something in a pan. It smelled good.

"Brandon, your dad says you have to go up to the field and feed the pigs as soon as you get in," she said, hearing them come in but not looking up. She was a lean woman with midlength dark hair, dressed in work trousers and a loose blue shirt. When she saw Mandy she looked surprised but wiped her hands on a towel and came over to say hello.

"You were over here the day before yesterday," she said. "When Ken had his accident." Her face broke into a smile, and the worried, overworked look vanished. "I'm glad our Brandon's got friends he can bring home at last!" she said.

"Mom!" Brandon snapped. He turned and stamped out of the room.

"Oh, dear!" Mrs. Gill sighed. "What did I say?"

Mandy smiled back. "Never mind. Nice to meet you, Mrs. Gill!" She thought Brandon's mom was a down-to-earth, friendly, busy woman. The little Gills were great. "Do you know where James is?" she asked.

"Here!" James appeared from a dark alcove, nursing furry little Harry in the palm of his hand. Angela emerged, too and kept the twins at bay as they tried to reach up and poke at the gerbil.

"James, let's go and help Brandon with the pigs!" Mandy suggested in a loud, obvious voice.

He nodded. But it took a few more minutes to get clear of the kitchen full of animals and children. Cheerfully they waved goodbye and stepped straight into a rumbling argument out in the farmyard. Mr. Gill had pulled up and jumped down from his tractor. It was parked against the double door of the barn nearest the house, and he was speaking to his son.

"It's not just the feed!" he said. He stood with his broad back toward Mandy and James, hands on hips. By the sound of things, Brandon was giving his father a good argument. He looked grim and determined. But Mr. Gill's low voice rumbled on. "You know it's the labor costs as well."

"Ken would work for nothing if you asked him!" Brandon said. His expression was surly.

"Don't talk crazy. How can he live if he's not earning?" his father said. "And then there's the space they take up!"

"That land's useless for crops!" Brandon pointed out. "Not with those rocks everywhere!"

Mr. Gill turned away, exasperated. He saw Mandy and James standing there and immediately his expression relaxed. He smiled.

Mandy was caught off guard. She was ready to hate Mr. Gill, Ruby's persecutor. She thought he'd be ugly and rough and hard-hearted through and through. She was ready to stand up to him. But he was smiling!

"Now, then!" he greeted them chattily. His face was weather-beaten and open. Only his long, straight nose reminded Mandy of Brandon's sharp, skinny build. Instead of Brandon's dark brown coloring, Mr. Gill had pale gray eyes under a broad forehead. His thick, light brown hair rose straight back and curled slightly over his small ears. Everything about him suggested steady friendliness.

He was dressed in shabby work clothes. His shirt was worn out at the elbow, Mandy noticed, and his trousers had a patch on the knee. All this niggling talk about the cost of pig rearing suddenly made more sense. They were short of money, she remembered. That was what made him seem hard.

As Mr. Gill clambered back up into the cab of his tractor, he stopped and swung around. "Did you do what I said?" he asked Brandon.

Brandon colored, still sore from the argument. He hesitated.

"That means no!" Mr. Gill assumed. "Well, it's no good putting it off any longer, Brandon!"

"Okay, okay!" Brandon backed off.

"You never listen to a word I say, do you?" He swung himself up into the cab, then leaned out sideways. "For the last time, you'll have to get rid of that runt!"

He started up the engine. He meant Ruby! Mandy and James joined Brandon to form a little cluster in the yard. They looked up at Mr. Gill in his cab as the tractor trundled past, shedding big clods of earth from its giant, deep-tread tires.

"I don't want to have to mention it again!" he warned as he sailed out of the yard.

Brandon had turned pale. He refused to look Mandy in the face.

"Don't worry," she said. "We'll think of something!"

"Well, while you're thinking about it, I'm going to feed the pigs!" he said shortly, too upset to stay and talk. "Back in half an hour!" And he was gone.

James stared at Mandy. "Ouch!" he said.

"Come on, let's go and check on Ruby," she said. "And while we're at it, we can be looking for somewhere good to hide her!"

They stepped in through the giant doors of the hay barn into the dry, sweet-smelling atmosphere. The barn was stacked high to either side with pale golden bales, built like bricks in an immense pyramid right up to the roof. Brandon had left Ruby in her box here in an out-of-the-way corner. They made their way through the semidarkness, ready to clean out the piglet's box and make her comfortable again.

Mandy climbed over a small pile of bales to the box, with James following. "Oh, no!" she wailed. The box was tipped over, the flaps wide open. Ruby had escaped! She gasped and stared back at James.

"Oh, no, what?" a little voice called from the doorway. A shaft of yellow sunlight broadened as the door opened and three small figures trailed into the barn.

"Oh no, nothing!" James said quickly. He darted glances around the stacks of bales. Ruby had vanished!

"Oink! Oink!" came a happy snorting sound from high in the stack above Mandy. She swallowed hard.

Angela led the little tribe of Gills into the barn like an intrepid explorer. "Is that a pig?" she asked inquisitively.

"Oh, no!" James said again. Alarm shot all over his face. He snorted and pretended to sneeze loudly. "Aaatchoo! Hay fever!" he said.

"It sounded like a pig!" Angela insisted. She climbed up beside James.

Mandy frantically searched the barn. Again she heard distinct little grunts from up on high. And, yes; there was Ruby's flop-eared face peering down and grinning from a high bale. "Chase me!" she seemed to say. She disappeared with a toss of her head. Mandy began to scale the pyramid of straw bricks.

James began to play the clown for the children out of sheer panic. He sang the only song that came to mind: "Whose pigs are these?" he yelled in a tuneless shout. He jumped down level with Angela and the twins. They stared at him in silent wonder.

He stopped to recall Mr. Hope's song—"Whose pigs are these... ?"

Somehow he had to disguise Ruby's snorts and squeals as Mandy tackled her up on a high ledge.

"... They are Jim Potts',

They're covered with spots,

And I found 'em in a supermarket wagon!"

Mandy heard the children below erupt into a chorus of giggles. She heard James sneeze and clown around again. And now she stared Ruby in the face. "Come on, Ruby, that's a good girl!" she whispered. She was breathless from the climb and she prayed that Ruby wouldn't take it into her head to leap, toboggan-style, back down the tempting slope of bales!

Ruby cocked her head and grinned. She stood poised.

"Here, Ruby; here, girl!" Mandy pleaded. If Angela caught sight of the piglet, news would be out in a flash, and Operation Saddleback would be over before it had begun! Mandy held her cupped hand toward the runaway, pretending there was a treat

hidden there. "Here, Ruby!" she said again.

The piglet fell for it. She came straight up, good as gold. Eating was more fun than escaping, of course!

Mandy smiled at the feeling of the soft snout on her empty palm. Slowly her other arm came under Ruby's belly. "Now, don't squeal!" she warned.

Ruby squealed, and she yelled and hollered. She wriggled and struggled and squirmed. Mandy held fast. Down below, James had entered into a loud game of pirates with the little ones. Their screams drowned out Ruby's, but only just.

"Avast, me hearties!" James roared. "Whaar be those landlubbers?"

Angela and the twins yelped with delight. Soon he tempted them out of the barn, swashbuckling into the daylight. Now Mandy could safely descend with Ruby.

She pushed back her blond hair and breathed easily again as she settled the piglet back into her battered cardboard box. Soon James returned.

"Talk about a close shave!" he gasped. "Anyway, they've gone in for a snack now. And Brandon's on his way back down from the field; I just saw him."

Mandy nodded. She fixed her gaze on the middle distance and frowned thoughtfully.

"You look as if you've had an idea!" James said. He

settled onto the hay bales to rest and catch his breath. While Mandy gave Ruby one last check, Brandon slipped in through a chink in the barn door. James waited for her reply.

"I have!" she agreed. They sat around in the dull light. "Now, listen!" she said. Their three heads came together. "I've thought of just the thing!"

Seven

"We need something bigger than a box, something that will keep Ruby warm and at the same time well hidden!" Mandy listed the points on her fingers.

Brandon and James nodded after each point.

She paused. "Well, do you know what's on the far side of this stack of hay bales?" she asked Brandon. When she'd gone mountaineering after Ruby, she'd glanced down into the dark, unused corner of the barn.

Brandon shrugged. "Just a heap of junk, as far as I know. No one goes around there much."

Mandy's eyes lit up. "Oh, good!" she said. "And you're sure it's just junk?"

"Yes, it's stuff my mom's thrown out. Old furniture,

toys, stuff like that. Only she won't throw it away in case it comes in handy. It never does. My dad's always moaning at her to let him throw it out." He looked inquisitively at Mandy. She'd picked up the box with Ruby in it and begun to clamber up the stack of bales.

"Follow me!" she said.

All three climbed to the top of the stack, taking turns to balance the precious box. At last they sat twenty feet up, legs dangling, perched on the summit. Mandy looked down on a heap of battered bicycles with buckled wheels and kitchen chairs with no backs or three legs. And back against the cobwebby stone wall, in a far corner, she pointed to an old wooden playpen.

"Isn't that perfect?" she cried.

James looked doubtfully at Brandon. "A piglet in a playpen?" he asked.

Brandon looked puzzled but interested. Ruby snorted inside her box.

"Careful with Ruby!" Brandon warned.

Mandy held the box in her arms and began to slither down the prickly stack, explaining as they went. "All we have to do is turn the playpen right side up, fasten it to the floor somehow so Ruby can't shift it, line the floor with good, clean straw, and there you are, a perfect pigsty!" She seized one corner and shook the playpen free of cobwebs and wisps of hay.

"That's the twins' playpen; I remember it!" Brandon said. The wooden structure was roughly five feet square; with railings about three inches apart. Beads that had once been bright yellow and red decorated the top bars. "It was Angela's too." He fingered the faded wooden beads. "And mine, probably!"

"But your mom's thrown it out, hasn't she? And it's just right for Ruby!" Mandy was busy setting it down flat in an area of floor she'd cleared of battered plastic cars and burst footballs.

Brandon looked around. "Nobody will think to come and look back here," he agreed. "And it's a long way from the house. No one will hear the noise. These walls are good and thick."

Mandy's hopes were mounting. She stood back and considered how to fasten the playpen to the floor. "We can anchor it with heavy stones from that pile over there," she suggested.

But James, logical, practical James, had an objection. "Ruby will be able to get through those railings," he pointed out. "At least until we've fattened her up a little. They're way too wide apart!"

"Oh, heck!" Brandon exclaimed. "You're right, she will!" His face fell. They were back to square one. "We'll never figure something out in time!" he moaned.

"Let's just check," Mandy said briskly. She opened

the box and spoke nicely to Ruby, tickling her under the chin. Then she picked her up and tried her for size against the railings of the playpen. Ruby squirmed and sniffed at her new surroundings. She would be able to slip between the railings with ease. "You're right," Mandy said to James. She saw that Brandon was disappointed, and she felt downcast herself. "What now?"

"Well..." James said slowly. He cast an eye over the tangled heap of discards. "Can you find us any good strong string, or spare rope?" he asked Brandon.

Brandon nodded and disappeared nimbly up the stack of bales. "Back in two minutes," he promised.

"We need to block up the gaps," James explained, as Mandy returned Ruby to her dreaded box. The piglet kicked and scuffed around inside. "She likes it better out here," James grinned. "And no wonder. Never mind, Ruby; we'll soon have the ideal thing for you."

"How?" Mandy asked. She watched James take a scout knife from his pocket, and with one of the gadgets he began to wrench away at the bolts attaching the battered bicycle wheels to their frames. Soon he had three of them free and lined up along the sides of the playpen.

"Now..." he said, thinking deeply. "What's this?"

He seized a wire mesh screen from the bottom of the heap.

"It's an old fire screen!" Mandy recognized the sort of thing they used to put in front of open fires to stop hot coals from falling out. "Gran and Grandad used to have one!"

James stood it alongside the playpen. Now all the open railings were protected, and Brandon soon came hurrying back with lengths of rope and another knife.

James and Mandy lashed the wheels and the fire screen to the outside of the playpen while Brandon weighted it down with six or seven heavy stones. After five minutes of pulling ropes, tying knots, and testing them for strength, the three of them stood back to admire their efforts.

"Not very pretty, is it?" Mandy admitted with a sigh.

"Who cares!" James said. "No one's going to see it, we hope. At least it's safe and warm and dry." He turned to Brandon. "What do you think?" he asked anxiously.

Brandon looked it over with a critical eye. He took hold of it and rattled it. He wanted to be sure that the playpen was the right place for Ruby. "I guess it'll do!" he said at last.

"Don't sound so pleased!" Mandy teased. She

grinned as she watched Brandon rescue Ruby from her cardboard box for the last time. He set Ruby down inside her pen. She lifted her feet and tested the straw. She looked around for beefy rivals and sniffed the warm air. Then down went her snout, rummaging for food.

"Uh-oh!" Brandon went quickly and opened a package of the food he'd bought at Animal Ark. "She's hungry!" He offered her a handful of pellets. She gobbled them straight down.

"Again!" James laughed.

"She's always hungry," Brandon explained.

"And she has a lot of eating to do," Mandy said, "to catch up with those hefty porkers on the hill!" She stood back again to admire Ruby in her ramshackle playpen. It was going to be fun helping to hand-rear a pure British Saddleback pig! If Brandon would let her, she'd come up to Graystones Farm every single day!

Ruby's new home proved a great success. The playpen was sturdy, stable, and easy to clean. The barn turned out to be a good hiding place for the condemned piglet.

Brandon told Mandy how his father had looked in on the pig field the day after they'd hidden her and done a head count of Pauline's piglets. Nine strapping porkers jockeyed for position around the sow. There was no sign of the runt. He'd nodded with satisfaction and found no reason to speak with Brandon about it again. It was dealt with. Brandon had been busy in the field doing the work of two men in Ken's absence. So Mr. Gill had given him a wave and walked away, well pleased.

Brandon kept the secret closely hidden. He took charge of Ruby's diet, while Mandy and James kept their promise to come up every day, bringing all their leftover vegetables in shopping bags. It turned out that cabbage leaves and carrot peelings were Ruby's favorite treats.

"How much weight has she put on?" James wanted to know. It was a whole week since the playpen had become her home, and Mandy and he stood admiring the plump little pig. Ruby basked in a narrow ray of sunshine, perched on a hay bale as Brandon spread clean straw in her pen.

"At least ten pounds, I bet," Brandon calculated.

"In one week!" Mandy exclaimed. She stared at Ruby's chubby face and squat little body.

"Let's see!" James did quick sums in his head. "That's about a pound and a half a day, and that's what she's supposed to gain, isn't it? We're on target!" he said proudly.

"We sure are," Brandon agreed happily. "She's just under twenty-nine pounds!"

James did more of his beloved math. "If more than two-thirds of the potential energy of the food pigs eat is lost, that means we should be feeding Ruby nearly five pounds of food a day!" he explained.

Mandy couldn't follow James's number-crunching point. "All I know is, she looks perfectly happy now!" she said.

"Pass me that food and don't just stand there!" Brandon, busy in the pen, pointed to one of the shopping bags.

James and Mandy made the big mistake of taking their eye off Ruby at the same moment. Together they went for the bag. When they looked up, Ruby's hay bale was vacant.

"Oh, no, she's gone again!" James's mouth fell open.

"Quick!" Mandy pointed to the narrow slit in the barn door. Ruby was heading for it, her little round rump and curly tail going hell for leather toward freedom. They gave chase, lumbering after her.

Wisely, Ruby made a sharp left turn out of the barn, away from the house. Brandon, James, and Mandy dashed into the yard after her. James even got one hand on her back with a low dive, but she slipped from his grasp like soap. She headed for the grassy bank that led to the river.

"Brandon!" Mr. Gill's deep voice called. He'd just emerged from the tractor shed. "Have those pigs been fed?"

Brandon stopped short, trying to pretend nothing was wrong. Mandy and James watched helplessly as Ruby made a clean getaway. "Not yet," Brandon admitted.

"Well, hop up!" Mr. Gill pointed to the tractor. "I'm on my way up there, so I'll come and lend a hand." He sounded cheerful. It was a friendly offer Brandon couldn't refuse. He looked long and hard at the others.

"Don't worry, we'll find her," Mandy whispered as Brandon headed reluctantly in the opposite direction. "At least he didn't spot Ruby!" She sounded more confident than she felt. Chasing a lively piglet through undergrowth without attracting suspicion was not going to be easy.

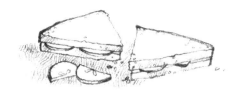

Eight

James and Mandy headed straight down the bank. They stopped at the river's edge and gazed both ways, up and downstream. "Which way?" James gasped. Lush green leaves sprouted along the banks—the perfect hiding place for a piglet.

Mandy took a chance. "Downstream!" she suggested.

Cautiously they took that direction, peering through the undergrowth, along the path, under rocks in the shallows, everywhere. "Ruby!" they called gently. But Ruby chose not to reply.

The late afternoon sun beat down on their backs and caught the clear, swirling water with dimples of bright light. Mandy squinted her eyes for a sight of the black-and-pink runaway. Ruby was as big as a decent-sized dog now, surely easy enough to spot. But they'd reached a bend in the river where it broadened. On the near bank was a pebbly beach for picnickers. And still there was no sign of Ruby.

"Should we turn back and try the other way?" Mandy asked.

James stood up straight and arched his back, stiff from all the crouching and searching in vain. "She has a pretty good head start on us now," he warned. It would be like going back and starting again.

Then a voice attracted their attention. "That's it, sit up nicely!" Its rich tones floated toward them from a secluded spot on the beach. "Good girls and boy; now you can have a lovely treat!"

Something told Mandy that this was a situation to investigate. "Mrs. Ponsonby!" she mouthed at James, and beckoned him forward.

"There, isn't that delicious! Yum, yum!" Mrs. Ponsonby crooned.

They saw her hat, a pink floppy one with a huge pink bow. They saw her broad back, in pretty floral pink. They saw a fine picnic spread out on a clean white cloth—sandwiches and doggy treats. There were Pandora and Toby sitting up on their hind legs, tongues hanging out. And there was Ruby, eyes gleaming, mouth chomping, patiently awaiting the next tidbit from the luxurious spread!

"We might have guessed!" James muttered. "Where there's food, there's Ruby!"

"She can smell it a mile off," Mandy agreed. But she watched with amazement as Mrs. Ponsonby selected a tasty cucumber sandwich and held it high in the air.

"Good girls!" Mrs. Ponsonby had scooped Toby up under one arm, but still she coaxed Ruby and Pandora. "Precious little friends! Such friendly girlies!"

Yuck! Mandy thought. She saw that Ruby and Pandora's eyes were fixed on the sandwich. They sat bolt upright, mouths watering.

"Piggy's turn!" Mrs. Ponsonby said. Delicately she offered the sandwich to Ruby, who took it with a grin and swallowed it whole. "Good girl, Pandora!" Mrs. Ponsonby told her patient pet.

Mandy turned to James. "Amazing!"

"That's another couple of pounds she's gained, at any rate!" he grinned. And they stood up, confident that Ruby wouldn't run away again.

"Ah, hello, Amanda! Hello, James!" Mrs. Ponsonby glanced up as they approached. She acted as if there was nothing in the least unusual in giving a picnic party for a Pekinese dog, a mongrel, and a piglet.

"Meet Pandora's new friend. A most affectionate little creature, and so well mannered!" She smiled down at Ruby.

Ruby cocked one ear and eyed them calmly. Mrs. Ponsonby fed her another sandwich. Gobble, and it was gone.

"Yes." Mandy smiled and fumbled for words. "As a matter of fact, we've already met," she said.

"Her name's Ruby," James offered. "We've come looking for her."

Mrs. Ponsonby looked crestfallen. "You mean you know her and you want to take her home?"

Toby wagged his tail, Pandora growled. Ruby snorted suspiciously.

Mrs. Ponsonby sighed. "Ah, well!" She flicked breadcrumbs from her lap. "All good things must come to an end, Pandora dear!" She leaned forward and scratched Ruby behind the ear. "Such a little charmer!" she cooed. Then with her free arm she grasped the piglet firmly around the middle, struggled to her feet and calmly handed her over to Mandy.

"Thank you," Mandy said, still almost speechless. "We were really worried about her."

"No need to thank me!" Mrs. Ponsonby smiled. She set Toby down again, adjusted her hat, and straightened the creases from her dress. "The pleasure was all mine!" Then she looked inquisitively at them each in turn. "Where does Ruby live?" she asked. "Oh, of course, I expect it's at Graystones, where else?"

Mandy had been ready to answer, but Mrs. Ponsonby gave her no time. "Well, that's quite easy for us to visit, Pandora dear; not at all out of our way!" She came up with the Pekinese and mongrel at her heels and tickled Ruby's chin. "We'll see you soon, my pet!" she promised.

"Oh, no!" Mandy said, then stopped.

"It's not quite that simple," James explained.

There was an awkward silence.

Mandy stared deep into Mrs. Ponsonby's round, powdered face. There was a puzzled, hurt look there. And suddenly everything poured out. "I'm sorry, Mrs. Ponsonby. Pandora can't visit Ruby because Ruby's not supposed to be there!"

Out came the tale of Mr. Gill's cruel death sentence, Brandon's loyalty to poor little Ruby, the search for a safe hiding place. "We've had to hide her away in secret to save her life! No one knows she's there in the playpen except us—and now you!" Mandy finished. She felt Ruby nestle against her and settle down for a nap.

There was another pause as Mrs. Ponsonby took everything in. "I see!" she said. "And you helped to save Ruby's life?"

Mandy nodded. But now that she'd started to talk, there was no stopping her. There was something else she needed to explain. It was what bothered her whenever she thought of the Graystones pigs. What would happen to Ruby later on, even if they saved her life now? She could never talk to Brandon or even James about it. "The trouble is," she confessed to Mrs. Ponsonby, "we may have helped Brandon to save Ruby's life, but for how long?"

"What do you mean, dear?" Mrs. Ponsonby's face was the picture of concern.

Mandy glanced at James. She felt the tears well up. "Well, she lives on a pig farm. And we're helping to feed her..." Again she paused. "But it says in my mother's book that when they get to about a hundred and ten pounds, that's when they're ready for... I mean, that's when they're taken to..." But she couldn't finish the sentence before the tears came.

"Fifty-three days!" James said in a hollow voice. The numbers clicked inside his head. "That's how long she has! Less than two months!"

"Oh!" Mandy cried. She clutched Ruby closer to her.

But Mrs. Ponsonby's face had changed. "Oh, my dear, don't upset yourself!" she cried. "There's something I don't think you quite understand! Do you think that David Gill farms those pigs to send them off to slaughter?" She squeezed Pandora and they shared a little joke.

Mandy looked up. That had been her silent fear all this last week—that Ruby would end up on the butcher's block. It didn't even bear thinking about!

Mrs. Ponsonby smiled kindly. "You have it all wrong, Amanda dear. Everyone in Welford knows that isn't the case! Ken Hudson tends many of those splendid creatures as show pigs. It's a small herd, just a hundred or so pigs, you see, and they make marvelous first cross animals for some of the less hardy indoor breeds—the Large White, the Welsh, the Landrace, for instance! He sells them for breeding!"

James stared at Mrs. Ponsonby. She was full of surprises today.

Mandy let the words sink in. "Are you sure?" she asked. "How do you know all this about pigs?"

The large lady came and patted Mandy's hand. "Listen, I've known Ken Hudson since we were children at school together. You pick up such a lot from just listening to him, you know. He's a marvel with pigs, poor man! He's missing them badly with that broken leg of his!"

Mandy and James nodded.

"He's convinced that pigs are intelligent

creatures, almost as clever as my Pandora!" she beamed. "They chose the Saddlebacks for Graystones because they're an outdoor breed. Many have a fine pedigree. They sell them for breeding. Believe me!"

Mandy did. She was overjoyed. She hugged Ruby and thanked Mrs. Ponsonby. She petted Pandora and beamed at James.

"Let's get back to the farm," James said. "And get Ruby bedded down for a good night's sleep!"

"And thank you, Mrs. Ponsonby! You've made our day!" Mandy cried.

They sped off back upriver. Ruby, happy to be carried, looked at the scenery with interest. Mrs. Ponsonby, Toby, and Pandora watched them go. "And don't worry, I won't give away Ruby's secret!" she shouted after them. "I'm sure she's going to make an absolutely splendid show pig after all!"

Nine

Mandy and James slipped Ruby into her playpen before Brandon got back from feeding the pigs. When she snorted and snuffled in her clean straw once more, they heaved a sigh of relief.

James watched her settle down for a snooze. "She'll probably dream of cucumber sandwiches!" he said.

Mandy laughed, but she jumped on Brandon when she heard him quietly enter the barn. "Why didn't you tell us?" she demanded.

"Tell you what?" Brandon noted Ruby's safe return and nodded once. He shoved his hands in his pockets and leaned against the wall as usual.

"That you don't send your pigs to the slaughter-house!"

"You never asked, that's why," he said simply.

"But we thought...we even thought that poor Ruby...well, you know!" She flashed a meaningful look at him.

Brandon shook his head. "If you knew anything about pigs," he said scornfully, "you'd know that the ones they send for slaughter are called baconers and hogs." He looked hard at Mandy. "You never heard me call any of our pigs those names, did you?"

"No," she admitted. "I just thought—"

"Well, you thought wrong," he cut in. "But at least you found her and got her back for me." He studied Ruby with an expert eye. "And you know what, I think she's coming along fine!"

Mandy blushed as she told her mother of her mistake.

They sat that evening at Animal Ark, watching a comedy show on TV. "Just imagine, I thought poor Ruby was going to end up as a pork roast!" she confessed. It was the first time she'd managed to laugh about it.

Emily Hope smiled gently and gave Mandy a small hug. "So much for jumping to conclusions," she told her. "You gave yourself a hard time imagining that Ruby's days were numbered. And there was no need after all."

Mandy pushed back her unruly hair and sighed. "Mom, did *you* know that the Gills' pigs were show pigs?"

Mrs. Hope nodded.

"Why didn't you tell me?" Mandy wailed.

"You never asked, that's why!" came the reply.

Even a broken leg and a fierce sister couldn't keep Ken Hudson away from Graystones Farm for long. One fine Sunday afternoon when Mandy and James were helping Brandon in the field, he came hobbling down on crutches to see his beloved herd.

"Careful you don't trip and fall and break the other one!" Dora Janeki called bleakly. She perched on the driver's seat of her Jeep and followed him with anxious eyes.

"Stop worrying!" he muttered, then raised one crutch in greeting. "Now then, Brandon!" he cried. At the sound of his voice, Nelson lifted his massive head and lumbered across the grass. Soon a stream of pigs of all sizes, but all hale and hearty, ran at him from every direction.

Ken scratched and tickled them each in turn as Mandy, James, and Brandon took a break from cleaning out the arks. They went to join him by the top wall. "You're doing a great job here," he told them. "I might as well hang up my boots for good!"

But Brandon wanted to fire a dozen questions at the old expert—about draining a waterlogged corner of the field, about putting an overweight sow on a diet, and about the strange behavior of another sow. "She's building a nest of straw, ready to farrow," Brandon reported. "But she seems really nervous about it. She won't let me near." He pointed to a solitary sow in one of the iron shelters.

"Oh, that's Sybil." Ken recognized her at once. "She's a gilt." He turned to explain to James and Mandy, elbows resting easily on the stone wall, his injured leg stretched out sideways. "That means this is her first litter. You'll have to keep an eye on her," he told Brandon. "She'll farrow in the next day or two. Try to be with her when she does."

Brandon nodded.

"Interested in a bit of work with Nelson?" Ken asked. He chatted on to Mandy and James as Brandon nodded again and went to get a stick and board from the field barn. "Training," he explained. "For the show ring. Nelson's our best boar."

"Oh, great!" Mandy said. She and James hopped up to sit on the wall—ringside seats.

"All right, Brandon! First off, just make him come to you and stand still!" Ken called.

They watched fascinated as Brandon slipped his left hand through a slit at the top end of a flat board about a yard square. "Here, Nelson, yip, yip!" he called.

The mighty black pig trotted obediently to him.

"Stay!" Brandon said crisply. He tapped the boar's rump with the stick and held the board flat against his flank. Nelson's ears flicked. He stayed put.

James turned to Mandy. "That's great," he breathed. "Next time I'll bring Blackie along and he can learn a thing or two about obedience from Nelson!"

For the next few minutes, Ken gave instructions to Brandon on how to handle Nelson's behavior in the ring. "He's a prize boar all right, but he's

headstrong," Ken admitted to Mandy and James. "He'll wander off if you let him, just when the judges might want to take a good look." He smiled fondly. "But he's never attacked another pig, even when provoked!" he said.

"Back, Nelson! Back!" Brandon cried. He tapped the boar's shoulder. Nelson retreated.

"See, he's a good-natured beast," Ken said.

Mandy agreed. She realized that Ken bore Nelson no grudge for the accident and was as proud as ever of his pigs. And she was looking at Brandon with new admiration. If Nelson or any of the other fully grown boars did decide to charge, that thin stick in his right hand was no defense, and the board would smash into splinters. But Brandon wasn't bothered. His quiet, kind way with them was all that was needed.

After a quarter of an hour or so, Brandon gave the boar a bruised apple from a nearby bucket and sent him off to bask in the sun. Then he came back to the group. "Well?" he asked.

"Good work," Ken said. "A little and often," he reminded him. "But you have something else on your mind, it seems to me," he said shrewdly.

Mandy looked at Brandon in surprise. He looked perfectly happy to her.

"I have," he admitted. "You're right." Then he took

a deep breath. "Ken, you remember that runt?"

Ken frowned. Mandy bit her lip and glanced at James. "The one your dad told you to get rid of?"

"Yes. Well, I'd like you to come and have a look at her," Brandon said. "Will you?"

Ken scratched his forehead, then hoisted himself upright on his crutches. "You mean to say you disobeyed your dad's orders?" he said slowly. "You never got rid of her after all?"

Brandon looked him steadily in the eyes.

Ken stared back. "Well, normally I wouldn't be able to go along with that," he said. "But since I'm laid off work at present and I'm not under any orders except the doctor's, I don't see why not!"

Mandy leaped from the wall. Brandon must trust Ken a lot, she realized, to let him in on a secret as big as Ruby! They all made their way to the farm, chatting and exchanging opinions.

"As a rule, I don't think the runts of litters ever catch up," Ken said. "Not in my experience."

"Just wait till you see this one," Brandon insisted. He held the wide wooden gate for them to pass through into the farmyard. "The vet gave me these special pellets for her, and Mandy and James come up every day to help," he told Ken. "I couldn't do it without them."

Mandy felt herself blush to the roots of her hair.

Praise from Brandon Gill! Ken smiled. James went on ahead, looking proud and pleased.

So Ken slipped quietly into the hay barn to take a look at Ruby in her playpen. She'd grown sturdier by the day, and more attractive, with her pretty pink and black markings, her soft triangles of ears falling forward over her blunt snout, her barrel-shaped belly. And now the piglet stood and preened herself, as if she knew she was on show.

"Well!" Ken said. "Very nice!"

"Isn't she terrific?" Mandy enthused.

"Pretty good," Ken agreed. He looked around the airy barn. "I think she could do with a bit of daylight. Is she kept indoors twenty-four hours a day?

"Except when she escapes!" James laughed. He told the story of Ruby's picnic.

"Scavenger!" Ken growled. "You've fattened her up well, at any rate." He stood back. "You know, Brandon, I'd never have believed it!" Then he hobbled around Ruby's pen to consider her from all angles.

Brandon beamed at Mandy and James. "He likes her!" he whispered. Then he joined his old master. "Tell me her good points," he insisted. "I want to know."

There was a long pause. Ken reached in and scratched Ruby's back. "Nice long back," he noted.

"Good growth rate. Very good. Lop ears, nice and soft and long. Good muscle quality. But not docile, you say?" He looked around at James.

James looked at Mandy.

"Does she do as she's told?" Ken repeated the question.

Mandy swallowed. "Not all the time. But it's just that she's very friendly!"

Ken nodded. "Well, that's good. I guess we can train her, can't we, Brandon?"

"Of course. So what do you think? Will she make a show pig or not?" he insisted.

They held their breaths. Ruby raised her snout and listened.

"I think she will!" the old pig man said at last. "In fact, I'd say she looks highly promising!"

That was praise indeed from Ken. They rejoiced in the hay barn as he made his way to the door, leaving them to pet Ruby and tell her how wonderful she was.

"We did it!" Mandy sighed. "*You* did it!" she said to Brandon. "Now your dad will have to admit you were right after all! Ken will back you now. When are you going to tell him?"

Brandon's face fell and he looked nervous. "I don't know; I haven't thought about it. Not yet!" He needed to get used to the idea that Ruby was a show pig before he tackled his father.

"Today?" Mandy was so excited she climbed to the top of the stack of bales and perched there. "Tomorrow? This week?" She fell over backwards and slithered to the ground.

James came sliding down and helped get her up. "You're covered with hay!" he said.

Brandon followed more slowly. "I think that's my dad I can hear out there now," he said. "Let's just act normal, okay?" He was set to lead them out.

"Act normal, James!" Mandy said, her spirits soaring. Ken's judgment of Ruby had sent them sky-high.

James roared. "You're crazy!" he told her. They burst into the daylight after Brandon.

It seemed that Ken had just reached the far gate when Angela and the twins spotted him and came clambering out of the house. "Who wants to sign my plaster leg?" Ken asked them good-humoredly. He took a stubby pencil from his shirt pocket. "Come on, Chris, put a nice big 'X' on the ankle just there!"

Now Christopher poked his tongue into his cheek to concentrate while Ken held his leg still and straight.

"Hello, Ken!" Mrs. Gill called from the kitchen.

And soon Mr. Gill came out to greet him. "Nice to see you out and about, Ken!" He shook his hand. "Do you have a minute?"

"All the time in the world, with this thing on my leg," Ken said. "What's it about, Mr. Gill?"

"There's something I've been meaning to talk to you about," he said. "It's been on my mind for a while."

Mandy felt Brandon's step falter. Something in his father's voice must have warned him. "Shh!" he said. They stood still in the middle of the yard. The shadows slanted deep into the corners. Wasps buzzed around a nest high in the eaves of the tractor shed.

"I'm worried, I have to admit, Ken." Mr. Gill went on in a voice almost too low to pick up. Ken looked deadly serious. "It's okay when the weather's dry like this, but when the rain comes, the pigs will soon churn everything up again. And there's that mess in the corner where the land won't drain." He paused. "What I mean to say, Ken, is that the field's pig-sick! I doubt if it'll support a healthy herd through this autumn."

Slowly Ken nodded. "Maybe," he conceded.

"You know it!" David Gill folded his arms. "We would have to leave it fallow for at least a year to let it recover." He shook his head. "A year without any use at all. Well, that's fine if we had anywhere to move the herd on to. But we're squeezed to the limit as it is. It's not like being on an upland farm like

High Cross and beyond. You know as well as I do that there's not an acre of spare land on this farm!" He sounded flat and final.

Mandy felt all her hopes dive to the ground. She hardly dared look at James and Brandon. Suddenly the shadows seemed to have lengthened, and she dreaded what was coming next. This wasn't just Ruby under threat! This was the whole herd!

Ken looked drawn and worried. He said nothing.

"You know what I'm saying, Ken?" Mr. Gill insisted. "It's the last straw as far as I'm concerned!"

The little man nodded. He looked briefly at Brandon, then turned. His crutches tapped the concrete as he hauled himself away.

"I'm sorry, Ken!" Mr. Gill called.

And Mandy saw that he did look dreadful. He was worn out with it, unable to look at Brandon as he hurried for the tractor.

"Wait!" Mandy caught hold of Brandon's arm. He swung savagely away from them all. "We'll be able to think of something!"

Brandon pulled free. He didn't want to speak to anyone.

"Let him go," James said.

They stood and watched as the yard emptied. Mr. Gill's tractor roared and lurched off into the fields. Ken Hudson hobbled slowly up the lane toward his sister's car. Brandon headed blindly for the riverbank.

Mandy and James followed at a distance. They found him kicking pebbles, picking them up and throwing them in wild arcs way across the water. He was thinking of Pauline and Nelson, Sybil and all the rest. It wasn't just Ruby anymore.

They left him and went sadly home.

Ten

In the dim predawn light Mandy woke with a start. The phone's urgent ring broke into her night's sleep. It stopped, and Mandy could hear her mother's quiet, calm voice making arrangements to go out on a call.

"Yes, all right, Mr. Gill, I'll be over in fifteen minutes," Mrs. Hope said.

Mandy shot bolt upright. Gill? Her mother had been called out to Graystones Farm! It must be something to do with the pigs, and it must be an emergency. Quickly Mandy slipped out of bed and into her clothes. "Can I come?" she asked. Mrs. Hope's face looked serious as she went downstairs to collect her bag.

Her mother's step halted briefly. She glanced back up at Mandy, then she nodded. "Okay. They want some help at a farrowing. We'd better get over there right away."

So Mandy and Mrs. Hope stepped out together into the still, gray world. In the field behind the house, a dozen rabbits bolted over the dewy grass as the car engine started. The sky was a flat, quiet sheet of gray.

"It's strange," Mrs. Hope commented as they crunched over the gravel drive into the lane. "I can't remember the last time that David Gill had to rely on our services at Animal Ark!"

Mandy nodded. She wished she'd had time to splash water over her face. "That's because Ken's usually there, and he's great," she reminded her. "The Gills wouldn't need help if Ken were there!"

"True." Mrs. Hope steered down the deserted main street and soon turned into the long, narrow lane leading to Graystones.

"Is this something to do with Sybil?" Mandy asked. "Brandon told Ken that she was nervous about her first litter. Ken said she'd need to be watched."

"That's right." Emily Hope glanced sideways and smiled. "Don't worry. It doesn't sound like anything we can't handle." She swung the car down the farm road.

But Mandy's stomach felt tight and anxious all the same. On top of everything else at Graystones, the money worries, the concern over the land, Ken's accident, and Brandon's long-term secret about Ruby, this last problem with the difficult births was making her feel sick. "Can I call James on the car phone, please?" she asked in a quavery voice.

Mrs. Hope looked at her watch. "It's very early," she said.

"But he'd want to be here." Mandy knew James cared as much about the pig herd as she did. He'd found he was good with these animals and had gotten really involved. Besides, she felt she'd like him to be here now.

"Okay, give him a call. See if someone will bring him over," Mrs. Hope agreed. "We'll probably need some extra help. David Gill didn't sound in the best of moods when he called."

Mandy made the quick phone call and was ready to leap down into the farmyard as soon as the four-wheel-drive came to a halt.

Mr. Gill strode out of the house to greet them. He looked grim and drawn, as if he hadn't had much sleep. Mandy noticed Brandon's figure hovering in the doorway. "We've just come down from the field," David Gill growled at them. "No change since I phoned. She's had two piglets, but she's stuck with the rest and I can't do anything for her!"

Mrs. Hope took this in. "All right. Should we all go across in my car, Mr. Gill? It'll be quicker." She waited for him to climb in alongside her.

Mandy climbed up onto the back seat. "Aren't you coming, Brandon?" she yelled. The engine already roared, and they'd begun to lurch toward the farmyard gate.

Brandon shook his head, his face tight and expressionless as a mask.

"Open that gate, someone!" Mr. Gill shouted.

His face like thunder now, Brandon strode across the yard and swung the gate free from its latch. Mandy, leaning out of the rear window of the four-wheel-drive, stared back at him. "Come on!" she yelled.

"What difference will it make?" he shouted back above the throaty engine roar. "He's going to sell the herd anyway!" And he slammed the gate shut.

Mandy felt her heart hit her boots. Sell the herd? He'd decided! What would happen to Ken? Where would Pauline and Nelson go? And what about Ruby?

The four-wheel-drive car bumped on over the rough, unpaved farm road. Mandy hung on, her knuckles white and her face drained of color as the sun finally rose above the horizon, a golden globe trailing wisps of orange cloud.

But then it was all action. They jumped down at the entrance to the pigs' field and went running halfway up the slope to the ark where Sybil lay. Mr. Gill and Brandon had put a farrowing crate into place—a rectangular iron frame with a platform where the pig could lie, to prevent her from rolling and crushing the newborn offspring. Two healthy-looking piglets lay close by, tucked into a deep bed of clean straw. But the sow herself lay hardly moving, and she rolled her eyes at their approach.

"See," Mr. Gill said roughly. "It looks to me like she's given up the ghost."

Mrs. Hope quickly assessed the situation. She knelt and felt the pig's swollen belly with the flat of her fingertips. "Still plenty of movement in there," she said, smiling briefly. "Now, in theory," she told Mandy, "she should be giving birth to around twelve piglets, one every ten minutes or so. If she's stopped, it usually means one of the unborn piglets is presenting itself in the wrong position. Let's see!"

It took her a minute or two to prepare to insert a hand and turn the awkward piglet around inside the womb.

"Why is it dangerous for her to stop?" Mandy asked. She knelt by Sybil's head and scratched gently between her ears. The pig sighed listlessly.

"Well, with this log-jam in here, it's very uncomfortable for the poor sow, for a start." Mrs. Hope concentrated hard. She explored the problem with gentle skill, trying to ease the piglet so that the head and front hooves could emerge first. "And secondly," she said, "the piglets could be starved of oxygen now, and we could have a lot of them in distress!"

Mandy shuddered and held her breath. She glanced up at David Gill, who leaned on the iron frame behind her mother. His face gave nothing away.

"There!" Mrs. Hope said at last. She knelt back. "That should do the trick!" She waited patiently, and within seconds Sybil had begun to cooperate again.

She pushed hard to help the piglet enter the outside world at last. Soon it wriggled free.

Mrs. Hope smiled. She put a hand under the piglet for support, gently wiped it with straw and then handed it to Mandy. "None the worse for wear. He's just got a lousy sense of direction!" She looked up at David Gill. "It's just as well you called me. The sow should be fine now, but I'll stay and see the rest of the piglets born, just to be on the safe side."

Mr. Gill nodded but said nothing.

"When did you realize she was in trouble?" Mrs. Hope asked. She stood and went to help Mandy arrange the three piglets closer to the mother. The little ones squirmed and tried to totter to their feet, tiny pink-and-black versions of the adult pig.

"My boy came and told me," Mr. Gill said, still looking on. "He was sitting with her all night."

"Brandon?" Mandy said.

Mr. Gill nodded. "He realized something was wrong, so he ran down to the house just before I called you. But, he's not here now, is he?" He looked out of the ark and down the field, shaking his head. "I don't know what's gotten into him lately!" he said. "But here's another helper coming up, at any rate."

It was James. Mrs. Hunter had just dropped him off in the farmyard, so he jumped the wall and ran up the field, arriving breathless and anxious. "How is she? How are the piglets?" he demanded. He hadn't even stopped to comb his hair or zip up his jacket.

"Fine now," Mrs. Hope told him. "They're all going to be fine, we hope!" She delivered the fourth piglet into Mandy's hands. "Come and see," she invited.

James came into the curved shelter and crouched beside them. His face relaxed into a smile.

"You're not squeamish?" Mrs. Hope asked. The next piglet was already impatient to be born, showing a tiny black head and hooves. She leaned forward to investigate.

"No." James held out his hands.

Mandy smiled at him. When you'd helped Lydia Fawcett deliver goats up on her hill farm practically in the middle of a snowdrift, how could you ever be squeamish again? "Good girl, Sybil! Well done!" she told the mother. Things were beginning to go really well now.

Mrs. Hope stood up for a break while Mandy and James snuggled the newly born piglets together, close to the sow for comfort and body heat. "You have a fine herd here," she said to David Gill, surveying the field. "They're a pleasure to look at!" Pigs rooted along a hedge in the early sunshine, or happily foraged through the damp grass.

His face lightened at the praise, but then clamped

into a frown. "They're more trouble than they're worth," he grumbled.

"Oh, surely not!" Mrs. Hope sounded surprised. "They're a hardy bunch, these Saddlebacks, and I know for a fact Ken Hudson is the best pig man in the valley!" She looked back inside the ark to see how Sybil was progressing, then she went on. "And your boy, Brandon, has done a marvelous job since Ken's been off. I mean, just look at the lovely condition of these pigs!" She smiled as a curious piglet from Pauline's litter came trotting up the slope to say hello. "Brandon has a way with them!" she insisted.

"Yes," Mr. Gill said doubtfully. "Maybe."

"Oh, yes, he has. After all, he saved that little runt, didn't he, and built her up to full strength!"

Her words fell into a terrible silence. Mr. Gill stood stock still, a puzzled look on his face. Mandy and James leaped to their feet.

"Mom!" Mandy rushed out into the open air. But it was too late.

"Saved the runt?" David Gill repeated with a deep frown.

Mrs. Hope turned to Mandy. "Didn't you tell me Ruby was fine now? She's put on all the weight she needs, hasn't she?"

Mandy had hardly ever seen her mother thrown

off balance by anything. She was always levelheaded, always in control. But now she looked flushed and awkward. Her hand went up to her mouth as she looked from Mandy back to Mr. Gill. "It's okay," Mandy said. "You're right; Ruby *has* put on all her weight!" She looked defiantly at the farmer. "She's going to be a fine pig!"

David Gill stared at her with narrowed eyes. "A fine pig?" He kept repeating what people had just said. "You mean to say Brandon never got rid of her?"

"I'm sorry, Mr. Gill, I thought you knew!" Mrs. Hope tried to step in. "He's done so well with Ruby, and he's absolutely devoted to her. Mandy told me yesterday that even Ken was amazed at how well she'd done!" She shook her head in apology. "I wasn't thinking. I just assumed you knew, too!"

Mandy closed her eyes. She saw how it must look; everyone in the world had heard Ruby's success story except David Gill.

"I'll give him a 'fine pig'!" he said, enraged. "Where is he? You say he never did what I told him?" He struggled to believe what he'd just heard.

"Oh, Mr. Gill, please wait a moment." Mrs. Hope held his arm. "Wait until we've finished here, would you?"

He shook himself free. "You stay here and do your

job," he ordered. "I'll sort out my own family problems, thank you very much!" And he strode away toward the bottom lane and his own parked Jeep.

Quickly Mandy beckoned James into Sybil's ark while her mother stood helpless outside. "Can you stay here?" she whispered. "Will you be okay?"

James nodded. "Why, where are you going?"

She took a deep breath. "Down to the farm, to warn Brandon!" She could see Mr. Gill storming off down the field. There was no time to lose. "We have to save Ruby!"

She began to cover the ground, down the rough grass slope, cutting diagonally across the field, hoping that running as the crow flew would get her back to the farmhouse before Mr. Gill's chugging Jeep.

"Mandy, wait!" Mrs. Hope called out.

She glanced back. James would explain. He and her mom would have to look after Sybil and the babies. She knew just one thing—she had to get to Ruby first!

"Brandon!" Mandy ran until her lungs felt as if they would burst. Her long legs sped over the ground. She saw Brandon fling open the farmhouse door as she darted into the yard. The Jeep still roared along the dirt road.

"Quick! We have got to get Ruby away from your

dad!" she cried. She caught hold of him and began to drag him toward the hay barn. Mrs. Gill and the three younger children had come to the door to see what the fuss was about. "Mom let it out by mistake!" she gasped. "Your dad knows about Ruby! Quick, there's no time to explain!"

Brandon grasped the situation. Ruby's life was in danger again. Some desperate feeling seemed to uncoil inside him. He shot ahead of Mandy through the barn door, scattering hay bales as he headed for the piglet's playpen.

They heard the Jeep engine die. They heard heavy footsteps in the yard, and raised voices. Brandon gave Mandy one last look, then picked Ruby out of her cozy pen.

"Stop! What are you doing?" Mandy shouted.

"I'm not going to stand by and let Dad get her!" he cried.

Ruby struggled as Brandon tucked her legs under her. He cradled her in both arms and began to run for the door. Mr. Gill swung it wide open and stood there in the entrance barring the way. Mandy ran after Brandon.

"Hold it!" Mr. Gill roared out. He put his arms wide.

But Brandon kept Ruby firm against his chest and ducked. He darted straight under his father's arms, heading for freedom with Ruby.

But Mr. Gill swung around and put out one leg just in time to trip them. Mandy lunged into him as Brandon stumbled and fell sideways. Ruby squealed. Brandon lay flat on the ground. He'd protected the piglet with his arm as he fell, but still she squirmed and hollered. He stared up at his angry father.

"Get up!" Mr. Gill ordered.

Mandy watched as Brandon seemed to hug Ruby close. Then he whispered goodbye. He loosened his grasp and set Ruby free. She looked at him, put her snout in the air, cocked her head sideways at Mr. Gill. Mandy heard the children come running. She saw Ruby shake her sturdy body, and Mr. Gill lunge forward to grab her.

"Go on, get going!" Brandon yelled.

Ruby reacted. She shot forward out of harm's way. But in her panic she'd lost her sense of direction. Instead of cutting left, down to the river, her little legs set off at terrific speed…straight for the house.

"This is it! This is the last straw!" Mr. Gill bellowed as he gave chase.

Angela, tousle-haired in her pink nightgown, watched Ruby head indoors. "There's a pig in our house!" she wailed. "It'll eat Harry! Oh, poor Harry!" She ran, arms outstretched, in her father's wake.

The twins thought it was fun. They held each

other's hands and went giggling after. Mrs. Gill looked down at Brandon. "Whatever's going on?" she asked.

"Ask him!" he yelled angrily. Mandy could see that he was battling against tears that had welled up in his eyes. His voice sounded broken.

She didn't try to say anything, but instead ran into the house. She left Mrs. Gill to comfort Brandon.

Inside it was chaos. Ruby had been backed into a corner of the kitchen by Mr. Gill. He held a tray as a shield against his legs and advanced, carrying a stout walking stick in the other hand. Maggie, the black-and-white collie, yapped herself into a frenzy. Angela stood on a chair holding precious Harry safely. Christopher and Lola peeped out from under the table. They yelled and pointed with chubby fingers every time Ruby tried to move.

"Here, girl! Here, Ruby!" Mr. Gill tried to rise above the chaos, tempting the piglet toward him. But Ruby wasn't fooled. She looked up at the stout legs and the tray and the stick. She backed further into the corner, behind a log basket. Mr. Gill advanced.

Then, at the very last second, Ruby shot forward. She came out of the corner, under the tray, straight through Mr. Gill's legs. For a stocky piglet, she moved like a cannonball!

Mandy gasped. Ruby dodged under the table. The

twins fell backwards on their bottoms. She leaped clean over a crouching, growling Maggie. She squealed as she scrambled wide of Mr. Gill's crashing stick. And she grunted in triumph as she reached the open door.

Back in the fresh air, her hooves galloped over concrete. She swerved around everything in her path—Mrs. Gill, Brandon, the Jeep. Her head was up and set for the far horizon. Her mind was on freedom.

"Stop her!" David Gill yelled. He came storming out to confront his son. "Don't just stand there like a useless lump! Stop her!"

Brandon held his ground. "What for? So you can send her off to the slaughterhouse?" He stood eyeball to eyeball with his father.

Mr. Gill took half a step back. "What?" he stammered.

"So you can send her to be killed, along with Nelson and Pauline and all the rest?" Brandon shouted. "You must be nuts if you think I'd stop her for you!"

"Don't you talk to me like that!" Mr. Gill seemed stunned. "I won't have you talking like that, you hear!"

Mandy saw Ruby leap and her rear end bob and vanish over the wall into the road. She headed uphill.

Far away, on the horizon, stood Welford's Celtic

cross, a local landmark. The piglet seemed to have her eye on it. She skirted to the right of the pig field and made her way over acres of young wheat, going hell for leather for the wide open spaces.

"Go and get her!" David Gill yelled, beside himself with anger.

"Go and get her yourself," Brandon said quietly. He watched with satisfaction as Ruby made her clean getaway.

Mandy didn't want to hear anymore. The argument in the farmyard became an uproar. She watched as two small figures emerged from an ark in the pig field, and she recognized James. She saw him spot the runaway piglet in the next field. He began to sprint after her.

No more thinking; Mandy closed her ears to the accusations flying around the farmyard. Ruby was the only thing that mattered now. She was a fast-disappearing black-and-white smudge in the green wheat field. Mandy too gave chase.

Ruby had no idea of the dangers she was headed for—cars on the road, hostile cows and sheep, careless people. "Wait for me, James!" Mandy cried. Her long stride began to cover the ground once more.

Eleven

Regardless of the dangers, Ruby knew a good thing when she saw it, Mandy realized. The little pig bolted out of the Gills' wheat field across the narrow road into a field of turnips. She stopped to root around for a tasty new snack, and Mandy and James came tantalizingly close. They crept forward, ready to pounce.

But Ruby gave a wicked wink and a small oink and slipped away through the broad turnip leaves.

"Ouch!" James yelped. He had to pick himself up from among the turnips, where he'd missed Ruby and sprawled flat.

"Come on, she'll get away again!" Mandy gasped. They'd been through many unusual times together, she and James, but never anything like this! "Don't make me laugh!" She doubled over with hilarity. James's hair was all over the place; his face was smeared with soil.

"What? What did I do?" he protested.

"You don't have to do anything. Just look at you!"

He stood and looked at her. "You should talk. Have you seen yourself?" he asked.

"Why, what's wrong with me?" Her hands went to her head. She pulled spikes of straw from her hair and burst out laughing. "This pig is going to get us into real trouble one of these days!" she said.

They ran on up the hill, chasing Ruby, who stayed well in sight about twenty yards ahead. She was obviously enjoying herself, even when she left behind the tasty fields and squeezed under a gate onto the heather-covered hillside beyond. Her spirit of adventure was undimmed.

"Where's she headed for now?" James gasped. The rough heather tugged at his feet.

Mandy glanced ahead. "The Parker Smythe place, by the look of things." She paused for a second, hands on hips. "Oh no, not the Parker Smythe place!" she cried.

The Parker Smythes lived at Beacon House, one of the poshest in the area, with its huge wooded garden and tall iron railings. Mr. Parker Smythe was easy to get along with, but his wife was standoffish and their young daughter, Imogen, was spoiled to death. Mandy knew that neither would appreciate a visit from Ruby. They put on an extra burst of speed, but so did the pig.

"Look!" James warned.

They saw Ruby trot up to the grand gates of Beacon House.

"They'll spot her on their security cameras," Mandy said. "Nothing gets past those things!"

Ruby peered beyond the gate. She saw two oak trees overhanging the driveway; grand, ancient oaks with a thick carpet of last year's acorns lying beneath. She considered the iron gate standing in her way; she licked her lips at the acorns. Mandy and James tried to creep up on her again, one to either side.

At that second, greed overcame the piglet. The acorns were too tasty to resist. Ruby pressed her nose between the iron bars and struggled to squeeze through the gate.

Mandy and James froze. "She's stuck!" James squawked.

Sure enough, Ruby had squeezed her head and shoulders through. Her front hooves touched Parker Smythe soil. But her pudgy hindquarters wouldn't follow. Her back legs pushed and kicked, her rear end jumped and wriggled, but it would not go through!

Mandy's jaw dropped. *Don't panic!* she told herself. *How do you rescue a pig stuck between iron railings?* She hadn't read about this problem in any of her mother's books. Ruby grunted. Her back hooves heaved and pushed.

Worse still, the front door of the house opened. Mrs. Parker Smythe appeared on the doorstep. Daintily she stepped down the drive in her slippers, head to one side, curious. Her daughter, Imogen, kept close behind, clinging to the back of her mother's white silk shirt. "Do let go, Immi!" Mrs. Parker Smythe said with a backwards swipe of her manicured hand.

Mandy swallowed hard. How were they going to explain this? Ruby grunted and struggled. James and Mandy stood up, red-faced, to confront Mrs. Parker Smythe.

"What is it?" The woman's head craned from side to side. Her eyes were squinting in a nearsighted frown. "Is it a dog, Immi? I don't have my contact lenses in yet. What's that stuck in our gate?"

Imogen stepped forward in her green-and-red school uniform. "It's a pig!" she announced.

Mrs. Parker Smythe flew into a panic. "A pig trying to get into our grounds! It can't be. Are you sure?"

She clung to her seven-year-old daughter as if Ruby were a tiger on the loose.

"Don't worry," Imogen told her. "I'll get rid of it." And she advanced on Ruby.

Mandy knew they must act quickly. If Ruby couldn't move forward, maybe she could squeeze out backwards. "Let's pull!" she said to James. They each took hold of a sturdy thigh and tried to ease Ruby out in reverse. It was no good; she was stuck fast.

Imogen towered above them on the far side of the gate. She was a strong child with a glint in her eye. "Oh, it's you!" she said to Mandy. "It's only the girl from the vets!" she called back to her mother.

Mrs. Parker Smythe tiptoed forward. "What a nuisance!" She regarded Ruby's loud struggles.

You might say "poor little thing!" Mandy thought. But sympathy for animals wasn't the Parker Smythes' strong point. It was no good to suggest that they try to ease Ruby gently backwards. They would probably shove too hard and do her some serious damage instead. "Just a moment," she stammered. "We'll think of something." She scrambled to her feet. "Maybe we should call the fire department?" she suggested to James.

But what goes in must come out, and Mandy reckoned that clever Ruby must have realized this for herself. The piglet suddenly stopped struggling and took a deep breath. She sucked in, and her flanks narrowed, her belly tightened. Now she was a slim, streamlined shape that could slip backwards with no trouble at all. She fell on her haunches and flipped sideways. She was free.

"Oh!" Mrs. Parker Smythe cried in a small, surprised voice, as if a firecracker had gone off behind her back.

"Serves it right!" Imogen said through gritted teeth. She laughed as James and Mandy threw themselves down on top of Ruby. The piglet squeezed out of Mandy's arms and fled once more.

James ignored Imogen's cruel laughter. "That was another close shave!" he said.

"A fate worse than death!" Mandy agreed. Ruby headed up the path, past Sam Western's farm. "Come back!" Mandy called. But her voice held a touch of panic, and the piglet galloped on.

"Now she's heading for High Cross!" James pointed ahead. They were both out of breath and their limbs ached, but little Ruby seemed unstoppable. She squeezed with ease under Lydia Fawcett's wooden gate and raced up the last stretch to the old stone farmhouse.

Scrambling after her, at the last moment they lost sight of her. "She's vanished!" Mandy said. They looked around the seemingly deserted farmyard.

"Oh, no!" James groaned. He sat down heavily on the edge of a stone trough.

Mandy stepped up to the house, searching every corner as she went. She knocked on the door. "Lydia!" she called. This time she wasn't afraid of the reception Ruby would get. Lydia was a goat farmer with a great way with animals. She was one of Mandy's best friends, shy but kind. And she had a down-to-earth solution for every problem. "Let's just hope she's found Ruby!" Mandy called back to James. "If she has, all our troubles are over!"

"Just for now, at least," James warned her.

His serious tone reminded Mandy of all the problems waiting for Ruby back down at Graystones Farm.

Then they heard a voice from the barn, firm and calm. "Steady, Houdini!" it said. "Stand back, boy!" Mandy and James followed the direction of the voice and peered inside.

Lydia stood patting her beloved Houdini's neck. The goat nuzzled her coat pockets and stamped impatiently. Then Lydia bent forward with a big earthenware dish full of rich goats' milk. Other goats peered over their stalls, black-and-white ones or all-black ones, like Houdini, with their curious, intelligent faces and green eyes. "Here now, drink this!" Lydia whispered to a breathless piglet.

Ruby! She cocked an ear and edged forward. Lydia looked up and saw James and Mandy. "Shh!" she warned. Soon the thirsty pig slurped at the dish of milk. "There!" Lydia said, satisfied. She ran one hand through her short gray hair, then stood back.

Mandy sighed with relief. The chase was over at last. She and James edged into Lydia's barn and closed the door firmly. They waited in the dim light until Ruby had drunk her fill. Lydia, dressed in her old brown work jacket and boots, smiled again. She wasn't in the least surprised or put out to see them. Gently Lydia bent down and gathered the runaway into her arms. "You're a long way from home," she murmured. "Now, James, you lead Houdini into his stall, please, and make sure the bolt is secure!" And she took Mandy and Ruby out of the barn across to the old-fashioned farmhouse. "And why are you two chasing this poor pig up and down the valley, may I ask?" she said with a quaint smile.

Mandy told Lydia everything. Ruby sat on Lydia's lap and seemed to nod her head at the important parts. "Brandon saved Ruby's life, that's for sure. But now he says his father will have to sell the whole herd because their pig field is no good anymore and they have no spare land!"

Lydia nodded and scratched Ruby's back. "So

you're worried about what's going to become of this young rascal?" She nodded her wise head and seemed to consider the problem, while Mandy stood up and paced the kitchen floor.

When James came in he offered another opinion. "It's too bad Mr. Gill doesn't have as much land as you, Lydia," he said quietly.

Mandy stopped by the small, square window set deep in the thick stone wall. She gazed out at the sloping pastures of sweet grass, clover, and buttercups where Lydia grazed her goats. An idea struck her straight and true. It seemed the perfect answer. She glanced at James, who nodded. She turned slowly to Lydia.

"This might sound like a silly idea," Mandy said, "But Mr. Gill once mentioned your farm. He said it had lots of spare land, like most of the hill farms these days. I wonder if you need all of your fields for the goats?" Her fingers were crossed hard behind her back. "He didn't tell me to ask you, Lydia. He's much too proud for that."

Lydia kept a firm grip around Ruby's middle and stood up. "Ah, I see!" She had the kind of warm smile that glowed and lasted. "No need for you to explain," she said shyly. "David Gill is obviously in a spot of trouble. He's a neighbor of mine, and what are neighbors for, after all?" She set off through the door, pausing only to grab a handful of brown envelopes from a high shelf. "Let's go down and pay him a visit," she suggested. "We may be able to help each other out, if it comes to that!"

Back at Graystones, the argument rumbled on. Brandon stood in the yard, facing up to his father. Mandy saw that her mother had finished with Sybil and her piglets and was now part of the farmyard discussion. She seemed to be explaining things to Mrs. Gill, who stood as usual looking worried and surrounded by little ones. Angela, Christopher, and Lola looked up anxiously at the circle of frowning faces.

"It would be a pity," Mrs. Hope said as Mandy, James, Lydia, and Ruby came within hearing. "Once you lose a fine herd like this, you never build it back up!" She sounded genuinely sad and only gave Mandy a brief smile of welcome.

Maureen Gill nodded. "Brandon's proud of those pigs," she agreed. "He and Ken win so many prizes at the local shows."

"That's right. And he's done a great job with this little lady!" Mrs. Hope gave Ruby an affectionate pat.

Brandon blushed as he took his piglet from Lydia. "Thanks," he muttered between clenched teeth.

Mr. Gill nodded silently but said nothing.

"I agree, David," Mrs. Gill said. "Brandon would be lost without them. What's more, Ken would be heartbroken!"

"I can't run a farm to save people's feelings!" he said roughly. "You know that. This is a business, remember!"

Mandy's hopes sank. Mr. Gill was stubborn. But Lydia cut in without waiting to exchange greetings. "It's not like making bicycles," she pointed out. "Or any other machine, for that matter. There's more heart in it than that, surely!"

Mandy could have hugged her for saying so. But would it make any difference?

Again David Gill nodded. "Morning, Miss Fawcett," he said pleasantly enough. But he stuck his chin out and looked grim. "There's no getting away from the fact that we're short of land here. No one can argue with that, can they? It's as clear as day!"

Mandy sidled up to Lydia. She knew how shy her friend from High Cross was. Would she be able to break the silence that had built up around David Gill? Everyone had tried their best, but he was still dead set on getting rid of the pigs. Ruby snuffled quietly as Brandon fed her an apple.

Lydia cleared her throat. "I know it may feel to you that I'm stepping on your toes, Mr. Gill," she began. "And that's not something I generally like to do. So please tell me to mind my own business if you wish."

Mandy stayed close by her. *Please go on!* she thought. *It's our only hope!*

David Gill stayed silent. It was impossible to read his thoughts.

Lydia continued. "My friends, Mandy here and James, gave me a very good idea just now!"

Mandy shuffled. It was typical of Lydia to include others in her good deed.

Mr. Gill glanced around the group. His head went down and he listened hard.

"They pointed out to me that I have plenty of spare land up at High Cross. Our hill farms are a good deal larger than those in the valley, as you know. Good grazing land. It's on the steep side, of course, but good-quality grazing nonetheless." Lydia paused "We think you should put your pigs out on one of my fields!" she said at last.

A gasp went around the group. Brandon looked stunned. He closed his eyes.

"At least until your land here has time to recover," Lydia went on. "It's a neighborly offer, Mr. Gill, and I'm sure you'll return the favor if need be." She looked him in the eye, tapped the bunch of brown envelopes against his arm and waited for his answer.

"What are those?" David Gill frowned and pointed to the envelopes.

Lydia sighed. "They're forms from the Department."

"The Department of Agriculture?"

"Yes. Forms for this, forms for that, forms giving me permission to breathe. I ask you, Mr. Gill, how am I to make head or tail of any of them?" Lydia risked a sideways glance at Mandy. "In the old days when my poor father was alive, we never had all this paperwork. Now if you agree to help me make short work of some of these, you're more than welcome to put your pigs up on my pasture in exchange!" She looked steadily at David Gill in a strong appeal.

Mandy watched as Mr. Gill stared first at Brandon, then at his wife. Brandon was standing still as a statue, hardly breathing. Maureen Gill stood with her hands clasped. She nodded gently. He turned back to Lydia. "It's a fair offer, Miss Fawcett," he said. "I accept."

The whole farmyard erupted. Angela and the twins scampered in among the grown-ups, cheering and laughing. Mrs. Gill squeezed her husband's hand. Then Mr. Gill went over to Brandon and clapped him just once on the shoulder. Brandon nodded back. For some reason, when Brandon glanced across and gave her a thumbs-up sign, Mandy felt the tears threatening to come and fought them back with a broad smile. David Gill had sided with his son at last.

Then Mrs. Hope came and gave Mandy a hug. "Well done!" She put her mouth close to Mandy's ear and whispered, "You've just seen a man swallowing his pride," she said. "And for David Gill that took some doing!"

Lydia had overheard. "We all have to do it from time to time," she said, sighing and shaking the detested envelopes in her clenched fist. She gazed around the excited group. "You'll make arrangements to bring the pigs up to High Cross as soon as it's convenient?" she said to David Gill.

"Yes, and I'll stop by to help you sort things out as far as the Department of Agriculture is concerned," he replied.

She smiled and fastened the top button of her jacket. "Well, I'll be off. Those goats won't wait any longer to be milked," she said. And she walked steadily away from the farm, back up the hill.

Mandy saw Brandon just once in school that day. He loped down the corridor toward her. "See you later," he mumbled midstride.

She nodded. He'd never be any good at offering invitations! "What time?"

"Five." He hurried on.

Mandy made sure that she and James arrived at

the farm on time. It was a gray day, cold for the time of year. "What's going on?" James asked. Brandon had met up with them by the river path.

"Come this way." He led them up to the hay barn. "Dad took a good look at Ruby this morning after you all left."

They gazed at the piglet in the playpen. She was a strapping half-grown creature now, with a friendly grin. "And?" Mandy prompted. She tickled Ruby's soft ear.

"He says she can stay," he said matter-of-factly.

Mandy nearly fell backwards with delight. "Don't you ever sound pleased about anything, Brandon Gill?" she cried. She and James jumped up on the bales and shouted. "Oh, well done, Brandon! That's fabulous!" They cavorted up and down the slopes of hay.

"So," Brandon went on, unruffled, "I figured it was time to try her out in the field again, and I wanted you two to be here." He picked Ruby up out of the pen.

"You mean she's going back with her brothers and sisters?" Mandy said. They followed him out into a gaggle of small children in the yard.

"Can we come?" Angela pleaded. And even Mr. and Mrs. Gill stopped work to go and see Ruby take her place in the field. The noisy procession headed up the narrow path.

"Look, here's Ken coming to see us!" Mrs. Gill pointed out. She waved at the distant, hobbling figure. "But who's that with him?"

Mandy recognized the pink hat. "Mrs. Ponsonby!" she whispered.

James clutched at her in mock horror. "And poor Toby and the dreaded Pandora! Lock up your animals!"

They marched on after Brandon, giggling and wondering whatever she could want now.

"Yoo-hoo!" Mrs. Ponsonby hailed them. She had a voice like a foghorn. "I've just brought along my friend Ken for a tiny visit. We were sure you wouldn't mind!" As she approached, she gave Mandy a broad wink. "Pandora was missing little Ruby so much!" she confessed. "But don't worry, I won't say a word!" She spied the piglet and stepped back in astonishment. "Ruby!" she exclaimed. "How you've grown!"

Mandy laughed. "It's time for her to go back in the field with the others, isn't it, Ken?"

The little pig man leaned on his crutches and nodded. "High time. And it's a great day for it," he said.

James looked up doubtfully at the gray sky.

"No, I mean it's a great day for young Ruby and

for the whole herd, I hear. Mr. Gill telephoned me with the good news about Miss Fawcett's field," he confided. "It's terrific!" His thin face wrinkled with pleasure.

"Look, Toby," Mrs. Ponsonby cooed. "Look, Pandora! Look at brave little Ruby!"

Brandon went on ahead into the field. He set Ruby down. Dozens of pigs came running down the slope to investigate. How would Ruby cope?

Mandy waited. The stream of pigs drew near. Ruby's head went up, and she didn't flinch. Instead, she planted her four feet wide on the earth. Would the others remember her as the runt and pinch, butt, and punish her as before? Would they resent her return? Steadily Ruby held her ground.

Half a dozen piglets came trotting forward. Mandy saw Pauline nose her way to the front, and Nelson lumbered after. They were so big, so hefty and solid. She trembled for Ruby.

But she need not have worried. Her brothers and sisters circled around her. She was easily as big as they, as round and firm and confident. The litter snorted out a greeting. One piglet sister gave her a friendly shoulder charge. Ruby returned it. Then Pauline came up close. She nosed the smaller ones out of the way and nudged her daughter's head. "Follow me!" she seemed to say. Ruby gave a little

leap and trotted off happily alongside her mother. Nelson nodded and grunted. All was well.

Brandon leaned against the wall and watched them go. He said nothing. The Gills were never going to be a family of many words. But Mandy knew that this was the happiest day in his life.

"I reckon she'll do," Mr. Gill said at last in his low, steady voice.

A warm glow washed over Mandy in the quiet, dull evening light. She and James had played their part for Ruby. The piglet made a half turn, nodded down at them, then trotted on.